Adventures in ODYSSEY

PASSAGES™

Glennall's Betrayal

Paul McCusker

D0954591

NELSON

Thomas Nelson Inc.
Nashville

to Elizabeth,
my wife and friend
and the mother of our darling son

GLENNALL'S BETRAYAL
Copyright © 2000 by Focus on the Family. All rights reserved.
International copyright secured.

Library of Congress Cataloging-in-Publication Data
McCusker, Paul.
    Glennall's betrayal / by Paul McCusker.
         p. cm.
    Summary: When he finds himself transported from
Odyssey to the country of Marus in another world, James
gradually becomes convinced that he has been sent by the
Unseen One to help a young man who is sold into slavery
by his jealous brothers.
    ISBN 1-56179-808-8
    [1. Space and time Fiction. 2. Betrayal Fiction.] I. Title.
PZ7.M47841635G1   1999
[Fic]—dc21   99-34006
                                    CIP

A Focus on the Family book published in Nashville, Tennessee,
by Tommy Nelson™, a division of Thomas Nelson, Inc.

No part of this publication may be reproduced, stored in a
retrieval system, or transmitted in any form or by any means—
electronic, mechanical, photocopy, recording, or otherwise—
without prior permission of the publisher.

The author is represented by the literary agency of Alive
Communications, 1465 Kelly Johnson Blvd., Suite 320,
Colorado Springs, CO 80920.

This is a work of fiction, and any resemblance between the
characters in this book and real persons is coincidental.

Editor: Larry K. Weeden
Front cover design: Peak Creative Group

Printed in the United States of America

00 01 02 03 04 05 QPV 10 9 8 7 6 5 4 3 2 1

A NOTE TO PARENTS
FROM FOCUS ON THE FAMILY

Adventures in Odyssey's "Passages" series has been designed to retell Bible stories in such a new and creative way that young readers will be able to experience them as if for the first time.

All the "Passages" novels are based squarely on key episodes of scriptural history. Anyone who is intimately acquainted with the Bible will recognize the basic outlines and spiritual lessons of the stories. But the names have been changed, the details have been altered, and (most importantly) the settings have been shifted to the land of *Marus* —an exciting world accidentally "discovered" by a group of kids from Odyssey.

Why this fictional device? Because familiarity can dull the impact of an oft-told tale. By "dressing up" the biblical stories in a new set of "clothes," we hope to release their inherent power in new ways ... and change young lives in the process.

This strategy didn't originate with "Passages." C.S. Lewis did exactly the same thing when he wrote *The Chronicles of Narnia.* Narnia was born when Lewis came to the realization that fantasy can be a particularly powerful tool for communicating gospel truths. "By casting all these things into an imaginary world," he once wrote, "stripping them of their stained-glass and Sunday School associations, one could make them for the first time appear in their real potency" (from Lewis's essay "Sometimes Fairy Stories May Say Best What's to Be Said"). This is exactly what we are trying to do with "Passages."

Parents should also be aware that, consistent with similar elements in the biblical accounts, these books contain occasional scenes of supernatural activity.

As has always been the case with *Adventures in Odyssey,* we sincerely hope that parents and children will read and discuss the "Passages" novels *together.* That's the best way to avoid misunderstanding.

Adventures in Odyssey Presents
Passages, Book IV

PROLOGUE

Whit's End stood waiting like an old friend. The porch stretched across the front of the Victorian-style building like a broad smile. The windows, like eyes, flashed in the winter sunlight. The melting snow hung from its head like a white beret.

John Avery Whittaker, or Whit as he was better known, mounted the steps to the front door. The winter wind gently blew his wild, white hair around his forehead. Jack Allen, his good friend, followed behind him with his head tilted down and his hands buried deep in his coat pockets. They'd just had lunch together and now returned to Whit's End so Whit could check on things.

The bell above the door jingled as they entered. It was early afternoon, so the booths and tables of the section of Whit's End that served as a soda fountain were filled with kids chatting, eating, finishing their homework, or doing all three at the same time. A hum of noise came from other parts of the building as well: the toy train whistle from the "county's largest train set"; a rehearsal of a play going on in the Little Theater; The Imagination Station at work upstairs; and the general noises from the many other rooms filled with kids, gadgets, and gizmos Whit had created to make Whit's End a fascinating place for kids to play and learn.

Connie Kendall, a teen who served as one of Whit's employees, stood behind the counter dishing out ice cream to one of the regulars.

"Hi, Whit, Jack," she called out pleasantly. She brushed a lock of her dark hair away from her slender, attractive face and up under her paper work hat.

"Hello, Connie," the two men said. Jack sat down on a stool at the counter, while Whit took off his coat to hang on a hook near the kitchen door.

"Where've you been all day?" she asked. Connie was naturally curious and loved to know what kinds of things Whit got into when he wasn't at the shop.

"Didn't you get my note?" Whit asked.

"No," she replied.

Whit's hand instinctively went to his coat pocket, where his fingers lightly touched the edge of an envelope. He'd forgotten to leave the note for her. "Oh," he said. An embarrassed smile formed on his lips but was hidden by his thick, white mustache. "I never got around to dropping it off for you."

"What did the note say?" Connie asked.

"Only that Jack and I were running errands."

"Errands?"

Jack swiveled off the stool. "Did you tell her about the

manuscripts, Whit?" he asked as he went around the counter to pour himself a cup of coffee.

"I mentioned them in the note."

"Which I didn't get," Connie jabbed at him. "What manuscripts?"

Jack explained, "A few days ago I found an old school notebook in the bottom of a trunk formally owned by Maude McCutcheon."

"I remember Mrs. McCutcheon. She taught English literature, right?"

"Among other things," Whit affirmed.

"Anyway," Jack continued, "the notebook had a handwritten story in it that took place back in the 1950s. It was about a brother and a sister from Odyssey who somehow traveled to an alternate world—an alternate dimension, I guess you could say—to a land called Marus."

"Marus? I've never heard of it."

"Neither had we," Whit said.

"I guess it was a really good story if the two of you were so interested in it," Connie observed.

"Actually, it was the first of *three* stories that we've been able to find," Whit clarified. "The first was in the trunk, the second was in Maude McCutcheon's study, and the third was being kept by Mrs. Walston, the mother of a boy named Wade who had slipped into Marus in 1945."

Connie held up her hand. "Wait a minute! You're talking about these people as if they're real."

"That's the strange thing, Connie. The people in the stories *are* real," said Whit. "We haven't been able to find the brother and sister from the first story, but the boy from the second story actually *lived* here in Odyssey."

"Really? Have you talked to him?"

"He died in Vietnam," Jack said sadly.

"Oh."

"And the *third* story was about Maude McCutcheon herself. She went to Marus back in the '20s."

Connie eyed the two men warily. "Let me get this straight. Are you saying you think these stories are true?"

Whit and Jack looked away without replying.

Connie giggled. "Come on, you guys. Just because someone wrote stories about real people from Odyssey who traveled to another dimension, that doesn't mean they really happened. Right?" She looked from Whit to Jack and back again. "Right?"

Whit shrugged. "I don't know."

Connie shook her head. "Mrs. McCutcheon probably wrote the stories herself or had her students write them as class assignments."

Jack sipped his coffee. "That's what *we* thought at first."

"Except that Mrs. McCutcheon didn't write them," Whit explained. "Someone called James Curtis did."

"We *think*," Jack corrected him.

"The handwriting in the notebooks and on his note to us are the same." Whit pulled a note from his pocket as evidence. "Whoever this man is, he's still living here in Odyssey somewhere, and he wants to meet us."

"Okay," Connie said, her tone full of disbelief. "So James Curtis has an amazing imagination, and for years and years he's been writing interesting stories about a make-believe place called Marus. It doesn't seem like such a big mystery to me. In fact, it sounds like you two are making it into a bigger mystery than it really is." She smiled at them. "Too much time on your hands, maybe?"

"Maybe," Whit conceded, smiling back at her.

Jack chuckled softly but didn't say anything.

"And maybe," Whit countered, "it's the *possibility* that the stories might be true that has me fascinated. I've spent my life pondering imponderables, asking the question *What if?* That's how I invented The Imagination Station. I asked myself, *what if* we could travel to other times and places to see what happened there? Whit's End happened because I asked, *what if* there was a place in Odyssey where kids could learn and have fun at the same time? Well... *what if* there is another world out there somewhere, in another dimension, and some kids from *our* world could get to it at various times for various reasons? Even if the stories *aren't* true, it's worthwhile to think about the possibilities."

"What do you think, Jack?" Connie asked.

Jack looked thoughtful for a moment, then affirmed, "I agree with Whit. I mean, I'm not convinced the stories are true, but it's been a lot of fun investigating them."

"I'm sure we'll know a lot more when we finally get to meet James Curtis," Whit concluded.

The bell above the door jingled again as a man in a blue uniform stepped in. It was Frank, their mailman. He'd always reminded Connie of the Scarecrow from *The Wizard of Oz* movie. "Special delivery," he said jovially. He dropped a large manila envelope on the counter.

"Thanks, Frank," Whit said and picked up the envelope.

Frank waved good-bye and was out the door again before they could say any more.

Whit looked at the envelope. It was addressed to him in a handwriting he'd come to know quite well over the past few days.

"James Curtis?" Jack asked after glancing at the script.

"Looks like it," Whit agreed as he tore open the flap.

"James Curtis sent you a package?" Connie said, then grunted. "If you ask me, he's probably some guy who's been desperate to get his manuscripts published and figured you'd be just the sucker to do it for him."

Whit smiled noncommittally at her. He pulled the contents from the envelope. It was a black school notebook with a white square in the center of the front and black tape on the binding.

"Another story," Jack said with obvious excitement. Connie thought his face, normally calm and passive, seemed to light up just a little. His blue eyes flickered and his cheeks flushed with anticipation.

Whit nodded and flipped open the cover. It was the same handwriting as the others.

"There's a note," Connie observed and pointed to a slip of paper that had fallen onto the counter.

Whit picked it up and read aloud: "Please read—and then bring everything back to me at 10:00 o'clock tomorrow morning, Hillingdale Haven."

"Hillingdale Haven?" Jack asked.

Whit's heart sank a little.

"But isn't that the mental institution outside of town?" Connie inquired.

"I'm afraid it is," Whit replied. His eye scanned the first page of the notebook. It was dated *March 21, 1934*. Under that was written: "The Chronicle of the Betrayed."

CHAPTER ONE

———————◆———————

James waited in the bushes until the black-and-white police car passed by. The two men inside were looking for him.

He waited, crouched like a small animal hiding from a predator. When he was sure the road was clear, he grabbed his bundle of goods—bread, cheese, and a slice of apple pie—and stood up. He adjusted the suspenders that were buttoned to his tattered wool trousers. His shirt, once white, was smudged with dirt and grass stains.

His Aunt Edna would scream if she saw the state he was in! She'd make him wash his face and comb his short, brown hair. But Aunt Edna was probably screaming anyway, he figured. Why else were the police looking for him? This was the third time he'd run away from her in as many weeks.

He gave his cap a tug and sprinted across the black tar to the field on the other side. The weeds were tall, almost like wheat, and would give him easy cover if someone came. He looked ahead to the forest that would provide his way of escape. It was about 100 yards away, across the sea of weeds that moved like waves beneath the gentle breeze.

It was a beautiful spring day, perfect for escaping Aunt Edna.

He was determined not to get caught this time. He had no intention of going back to Aunt Edna and her strict ways. She was a cruel ogre as far as he was concerned, and no law or lectures could persuade him otherwise. When his parents were still alive, they never made him wear the awful clothes she made him wear. Or forced him to read all those books. Or

8

made him do sums and fractions. Or dragged him to church every Sunday morning. His parents let him do what he wanted.

"You don't understand what it's like," he had said to her during their last argument.

"But I *do*, child," she replied.

But how could she understand what it was like to have your parents lose all their money and their home in this thing called the Great Depression? How did she know what it was like to be left behind with *her* while they packed his two sisters off to nicer relatives around the country? What made her think she knew how it felt when the news came that they'd been killed in a bus crash on their way to California? Killed while going to find work; while going to find a new home; while going to find *life*.

"You don't know! You *can't!*" James had shouted at her, slamming the door to his bedroom as a punctuation mark.

Later, when she had gone out to shop, he had collected his belongings: a torn photo of his family that he shoved into his trouser pocket and his father's ring—given to him after the accident, of course—which he tied on a string and put around his neck. After wrapping up the food in a rag in case he got hungry later, he had slipped out the back door, crept down the alley to avoid the tattletale eyes of the neighbors, and dashed away from the musty, old houses.

James wasn't sure where he'd go. Maybe he could find his two sisters, and then they could all escape together. Maybe they could start a new life in California as their parents had wanted. Maybe—

A horse's whinny caught James's attention. He looked in the direction of the sound—over there near the woods—and was surprised to see not only one horse but two, and a couple of wagons, at the edge of the trees. The wagons were large and enclosed, with doors at the back and windows on the sides that were shuttered. James had seen similar wagons when his parents took him to the circus a few years before.

Hope rose in his chest. Maybe a circus had come to a town nearby. Maybe he could join it and travel all over the country!

As if to affirm his hope, a man dressed in an odd costume rounded one of the wagons. He wore a shirt with a rainbow of colors going up and down both sides of it, and he had knee breeches and long, white stockings and black boots. He walked up to a large campfire and began to kick dirt on it, as if to put out the flames.

Funny, James thought, *the horses, the wagons, and the campfire all look like they've been here a while. But I didn't notice any of them when I started across the field. How did I miss them—or that mist that's moved toward me from the forest?*

It was strange to have mist like that in the middle of a sunny spring day. Yet somehow the mist didn't mute the colors of the scene. The green grass, the rainbow colors of the man's shirt, and the remains of the fire were all so vibrant, as if they'd been hand-painted on glass, like stained-glass windows in a church.

It had gotten noticeably cooler in the past few minutes, though, and James's skin went goose-pimply.

The weirdly dressed man spotted James and stood watching him. James started walking toward him.

"Hello," James said when he was close enough to the man to be heard.

"Hail," the man replied in a deep, resonant voice. He was a dark-skinned fellow with black hair, a thin, black mustache, and a gold earring in his left ear. His eyes were bright and piercing. He looked like the picture of a gypsy James had once seen. "What brings you to us?" the man asked.

"I was walking across the field and saw you," James said,

then abruptly added, "Are you a gypsy?"

"Gypsy?" the man asked.

"Or part of a circus?"

The man looked perplexed, as if James had used words that made no sense. He said, "We are traders. Are you here on an errand? Perhaps you are a message boy for someone who wishes to do business with us?"

James didn't understand what the man was saying either. "No. I'm by myself," he replied.

"Pity."

"Are you going to Odyssey?"

A puzzled expression spread across the man's face. "Odyssey?"

"The town near here."

The man shrugged indifferently. "We are going up the mountain, if that is what you mean."

"Mountain? What mountain?"

The man gestured toward the mist-covered woods.

James was truly confused now. No mountain stood behind those woods. Any mountains the man expected to find were in the other direction.

Suddenly a young woman came around from the back of the wagon. "We are ready, Papa," she said, then saw James. "Oh."

James was taken aback by her appearance. She had wild, dark hair barely contained by a red scarf. She wore a torn peasant dress that hung loosely from her shoulders. But her eyes really caught his attention: dark and piercing, just like her father's. James thought she may have been the prettiest woman he'd ever seen.

"Who is this?" she asked the man.

"Some boy," he said and began to kick dirt at the fire again. "I want to make sure this fire is out. It wouldn't do to be blamed for burning down the mountain. Connam would have us imprisoned."

"Or one of his sons would execute us."

"All the same."

The young woman turned her attention to James. "Why do you linger, boy?" she asked. "What do you want?"

James was going to say he didn't want anything. He changed his mind when he suddenly heard car tires screeching to a halt behind him. He spun around and felt his heart jump into his throat as he saw, through the mist, a police car on the road. Two officers climbed out and pointed in his direction. One called out to him.

"Oh, no," James gasped.

"What is the matter with you?" the young woman asked, craning her neck to see what he was looking at.

"The police. I can't let them catch me," James cried as he tried to think of what to do. The woods. They were his best hiding place, he thought.

The young woman looked at James. "The po-*what?*"

"The police! I ran away from my Aunt Edna, and they'll take me back." James watched as the two officers stepped into the field and made their way quickly toward him. "See?"

The young woman looked at James, then followed his gaze across the field. "I see nothing but a field in the sunshine."

"Sunshine! What about the mist?" James exclaimed. It engulfed him now, so that the police came in and out of view. One second he could see their badges flickering in the waning light, their batons swinging from their belts against their legs. The next second, they were lost in a gray curtain. "I have to hide," he said, then ran toward the woods. Ducking behind the largest tree he could find, he waited. He hoped they hadn't seen where he went.

James heard the young woman say in a pleading voice, "Papa!"

"No," the man said, stamping out the last of the fire. "We don't have time for children who are not right in the head."

"Papa, please."

"He's not one of your stray puppies, Fantya."

"You heard him. He needs our help."

"From what? He talks about mist when it is clear and sunny. He uses words that make no sense. *Po-leese*. What does it mean?"

James ventured a peek around the tree. The officers still hadn't arrived. Maybe they were lost in the mist.

"Papa, *please?*" the young woman said softly.

The man sighed. "We can take him as far as Dremat," he offered, sounding like a man who had lost this argument many times before. "He could run away from there, if that's what he wants. Does that satisfy you?"

"Yes, Papa. Thank you." Fantya turned and approached James at the tree. "Boy?"

"Go away," James said in a harsh whisper as he ducked behind the tree again. "I don't want them to know where I am."

Fantya waved a hand toward the field. "There is no one there."

"They're in the mist."

"There is no mist," she said firmly. "Look."

James cautiously peered around the tree again. His mouth fell open in astonishment.

The mist was gone.

The police—and their car—had vanished.

CHAPTER TWO

James stared at the open field, bright golden in the sunlight. All the colors suddenly seemed much more vivid than he'd ever seen before—the blue of the sky a much deeper blue, the green of the trees a far more intense green, and the yellow of the weeds almost shining. But the police were nowhere to be found. "What happened to them?" he asked as he stepped from behind the tree to look more closely.

"You must be hungry, perhaps feverish," the young woman said. "Come into the wagon and I will find you a portion of something to eat."

"A *small* portion!" the man shouted.

"But they were there," James protested. "Their car was on the road and—" James stopped suddenly. The road, which he could see from the field only a moment ago, had also disappeared. "What happened to the road?" he cried out.

Fantya and her father watched curiously as James ran across the field. Finally he stopped and gestured wildly to the ground, shouting back to them, "It was here! I just ran across it! Where did it go?" He paced back and forth, looking down at the ground like someone who'd lost a valuable coin.

"If we leave now, he may not be able to catch up with us," the man said.

Fantya gave him a disapproving look. "Now, Papa," she said, "he is obviously in distress. Look at the poor boy."

The man grunted and began to hitch the horses to the wagons.

James was grateful to Fantya and Visyn, her father, for the food they gave him and the ride they offered to the nearest town. His confusion was compounded, though, when they told him repeatedly that the nearest town wasn't Connellsville, as he thought, but a large trading town called Dremat.

"What happened to Connellsville?" he asked as Visyn snapped the reins and the horse lurched forward.

"The same thing that happened to your mystery road," Visyn grumbled. "*Poof.* Vanished."

They set off on a rocky road leading up a mountain, for there really was a mountain. And try as he might, James couldn't figure out where the mountain had come from—any more than he could figure out how the road had disappeared.

The other wagon was driven by a man called Nosz who had a thick, dark beard. Visyn's friend and business partner, Nosz was large and barrel-chested and wore clothes like Visyn's, except that he also wore a vest with bangles that dangled from the seams and jingled when he moved. Fantya sat next to Nosz on the front bench of his wagon. James couldn't help but glance back at her often, and when he did, he noticed by the way Nosz spoke and acted toward Fantya that he liked her a lot. She didn't seem interested in him, however, which made Nosz pout and complain like a spoiled child.

"Why do I waste my time with you?" James heard Nosz say to her once when they stopped to tend to the horses.

"I never asked you to waste your time," Fantya replied. "You are welcome to leave whenever you want."

Nosz growled and stormed off into the gathering sunset.

Fantya turned to James and wiggled a finger at him. "Come with me," she said. "There is someone you haven't met." She led James around to the back of the lead wagon and opened the door. "Go in," she ordered.

James climbed the small steps and went through the door into the dark interior. When his eyes had adjusted to the dimness a minute later, he saw that the inside of the wagon was decorated like a small sitting room. There was a cushioned chair and a small end table with a lacy covering and an oil lamp on top. He noticed a large, open trunk with clothes and blankets inside. A wash table sat under a shuttered window. A long, comfortable-looking sofa stretched along the front. In the corner sat a potbellied stove, its flue pipe jutting up and disappearing through the roof. The walls were a deep brown, and the floor had a faded carpet that might have been red once.

What really caught James's attention, however, was a large cot covered with huge pillows and ornately colored blankets. A woman—an older version of Fantya—rested on the cot, smiling gently at him. James took off his cap out of respect.

"This is your stray boy?" the woman asked Fantya.

"His name is James."

The woman waved James forward. "Come into the light. Let me see you."

James moved closer to the cot. The light from a lamp next to the cot splashed white and orange onto the woman's smooth face. She looked frail, but her eyes were sharp and clear.

"She is Deydra, my mother," Fantya said.

"A pleasure to meet you." James bowed his head politely.

The woman gazed at him from head to foot. "Your clothes are unusual," she observed. "I have never seen such long breeches. Or short boots. Or straps." She waved a bejeweled finger at his chest.

"They're my suspenders."

"Come closer," she said. "Let me see your face."

James obliged her.

Gazing at him, the woman's face suddenly lit up with surprise. "Your eyes!" she said.

"What's wrong with them?" he asked.

"They are two colors, blue and green."

"My eyes are brown," James insisted.

"Are you saying I cannot see? One is blue and the other is green," Deydra maintained. She reached behind her to the end table and picked up a gold-handled mirror. She held it up so James could see his reflection.

James looked closely. There was his slender face, the freckles that dotted his nose, and his eyes. He gasped. It was true! One eye was green and the other was blue.

"But ... how did this happen?" he asked. "Honest, lady, I looked in the mirror at my Aunt Edna's this morning, and my eyes were still brown. Like shoe polish, my dad used to say. I would've seen if they'd changed colors."

"Sit down," Deydra said.

Fantya brought a chair forward for him. He sat down slowly, still clutching the mirror and staring at his eyes.

Deydra leaned back against her propped-up pillows. "I have heard legends of strangers with eyes like yours or strange-colored hair. I have scarcely believed them. Why should I? I have never in my life seen such things. They were legends, that's all—stories people told around campfires to scare one another."

James was speechless. He barely heard what the woman was saying. His eyes. How had they changed colors?

"You've never told me about those legends," Fantya said, disappointed.

"They are not *our* legends," Deydra said. "We Palatians don't believe in the stories of Marus. But I have heard them in our dealings with this country. Now and again someone will whisper of the Unseen One and of His messengers. People with strange-colored eyes that do His bidding. And they say it was a boy with strange-colored hair who brought the illness that destroyed the world hundreds of years ago."

"Are you a messenger for the gods?" Fantya asked James.

"The gods?"

Deydra corrected Fantya: "Not *gods*, silly girl. The *Unseen One.*"

James was bewildered. "I don't know what you're talking about."

Deydra studied him for a moment. "Tell me where you are from."

James obeyed. For some time, he told Deydra about his father and mother and how he'd been sent to stay with his Aunt Edna in Odyssey and how much he disliked her and how he kept running away to find his two sisters and take them somewhere so they could start over again as a family.

Deydra listened earnestly, then probed him with questions about his "homeland." Over the next hour, James found himself trying to explain things like cars and policemen and electricity and planes. He didn't notice when Fantya slipped out of the wagon, and he barely noticed the jolt and rocking of the wagon as they continued their journey up the mountain.

"You are either a clever liar, a very gifted storyteller, or from another world," Deydra said when James had run out of things to say. "Which is it?"

"I'm not lying," James said.

"Then you have been telling me stories?"

"No," he said firmly. "I'm not making it up."

"Then ..." she hesitated, giving James enough time to draw his own conclusion.

James suddenly laughed. "I'm not from another world," he said. "I *can't* be."

"What you have described sounds nothing like *this* world, I can assure you."

James couldn't decide what to do. The woman didn't seem insane. But what was he supposed to think when she talked about other worlds?

"If I'm from another world, then where am I now?" he asked.

"At the moment, you are in the land of Marus."

"Never heard of it."

"But you're here."

"I don't believe it."

Deydra quickly reached over and pinched James's arm. He jerked backward and cried out, "Hey, what's the big idea? What was that for?"

"To make sure you aren't dreaming."

A small, red welt formed where she had pinched him. "This is nuts," he said as he rubbed his arm. "How could I go to another world? I'm not Flash Gordon. I didn't get in one of those rocket ships to the moon. I was running across the field."

"Fantya told me you saw a mist that no one else saw."

"Yeah, so?"

"Perhaps it was an enchanted mist. A mist that carried you to this land."

"I don't believe it," James said adamantly, his jaw set.

"Then go away," she responded angrily, waving a hand as if to dismiss him. "If you do not believe, why should I? What is to stop me from deciding that you are out of your mind or delirious with a fever that has changed the color of your eyes? By rights, I should throw you from this wagon and let you make your own way. Or better still, I could turn you in to the authorities at Dremat. They have places for people who have gone insane."

"But I'm not insane!"

"Then stop arguing with me and listen," she said, then softened her tone. "You are here. This much we can't deny. By your own confession, you do not know anything about this land. Sit and keep your mouth closed and I will tell you the way of things."

James noticed then that he'd wrung his cap like a wet dishrag.

"Unlike my own country of Palatia, Marus is not ruled by a king but is a collection of fiefdoms," the woman began. "Some families who emerged from the ashes of the previous world, the world that existed before the Great Catastrophe, have secured and maintained their positions of power. Some have become slaves. Some even disappeared completely. The powerful families rule what can be ruled of Marus. They negotiate the peace with one another and conduct business with the neighboring countries. This is why we travel from Palatia to the southern part of Marus. We trade with the family that owns the land, this mountain, the forests, and the mines of the south: the family of Connam."

The woman talked on and on. And James, feeling as if he were listening to Aunt Edna again, struggled hard to concentrate. But his mind kept returning to one thought: *How am I going to get out of here?*

Eventually he asked permission to let some air into the musty, old wagon. He opened the shutter on one of the windows, and the cool smell of pine blew in. He breathed deeply.

Standing at the window, James looked at Deydra and wondered how someone so sweet could be so completely mad. To think that he'd somehow stumbled from one world to another was ... well ... more than he was willing to believe. He didn't care what she said about Marus or who was in charge or legends about Unseen Ones or whatever else she made up.

He wondered what would happen if he suddenly made a break for the door and ran off. Would they come after him? Probably not. What was he to them? Just a runaway boy. That's all he was to anyone.

James checked the path to the door. Nothing stood in his way. The frail woman couldn't grab for him. His muscles tensed throughout his body. He could do it. He *should* do it. What was the use of staying here with these people?

He glanced out the window. If they were on a mountain, it would be foolish to leap out the door and roll off a cliff. He saw the dirt road and thick trees off to the side. His eyes wandered through the branches to the terrain beyond. It was dark now and hard to see, making him realize they had talked away the day, but he could still make out the upward slope. Suddenly, the wagon passed a clearing in the trees, and James saw a valley in the distance below. He thought he could make out the flickering lights of a town. Then he became aware of a great light that shone pale across the entire scene. His eyes turned up to the night sky, and instantly he felt as if someone had struck him in the chest with a sledgehammer.

"No!" he whispered.

"What's wrong, boy?" Deydra asked.

James couldn't speak. Even if he could've, he wouldn't have known the words to say. But in that moment, he realized the woman wasn't out of her mind after all. Neither was he, for his own eyes couldn't deny what he was seeing at that very moment.

There, high above him, was a sky with *two moons*. One was large and white, and the other was about half the size and slightly more orange.

CHAPTER THREE

———⊹———

James lay buried in a makeshift bundle of blankets and furs under the dazzling night sky. A roaring campfire crackled nearby. Only an hour before, the caravan had sat down to a meal of rabbit and potatoes. After that, Visyn had gone into the wagon to sleep, and Fantya had decided to take a late-night walk. James wasn't sure what had become of Nosz. He'd been silent and grumpy since they'd set up camp.

James tried to sleep, but his head kept spinning with all that had happened that day. The cool mountain air, the smell of the pine needles, the sounds of the night birds, and the glow of those two moons only made him more awake.

They were camped on Arinshill, the mountain nearest Dremat. Deydra had explained that the mountain was named after Arin, a prophet from the Unseen One who had heralded the Great Catastrophe. Only he and his family had survived the tragedy, and they were then led to this place by the Unseen One. There the world began anew.

James puzzled over the legends of the Unseen One. It seemed to him that they were very similar to the stories in his world about God. Were they one and the same? And what did the stories have to do with him, his different-colored eyes, and his presence in this strange place?

James again considered running away, but he knew now that he was a total stranger, a foreigner to everything in this world, and had nowhere to go. Staying close to Deydra, Fantya, and Visyn was the smartest thing to do for the time being. He hoped that going into Dremat tomorrow would help him figure out how to get back to Odyssey.

Nearby, he now heard the deep voice of Nosz. Then Fantya spoke back to him. She sounded angry. James waited and listened. Then he heard the distinct sound of a slap, open hand on skin. Had Fantya slapped Nosz across the face?

Fantya suddenly laughed—a low, humorless laugh. It faded away.

Nosz's voice echoed through the woods like an erupting volcano. "I've had enough of this!" he shouted. "Do you hear me? Enough!"

James froze as he heard the heavy thuds of Nosz's approaching footsteps. He came nearer and nearer, then stopped next to James. James cautiously looked up. Nosz peered down at him, his nostrils flared, sweat beaded on his forehead, his mouth curled into a sneer.

"What are you looking at, boy?" Nosz demanded.

James stammered, "Nothing, sir."

Nosz snorted and strode off.

James lay still, wishing for sleep, but also wishing someone would sit down and explain to him what all these things meant. He felt an ache in his heart, the same ache he'd felt when he was told his parents were dead. It was an ache of loneliness, an emptiness in the middle of his chest.

To distract himself from the feeling, he went back to the muddle of questions cycling around in his brain. How did his eyes change colors? How did he get into this strange country? How could he get back to Odyssey, *if* he could get back at all?

Eventually, the crackling of the campfire and the warmth of the bundle helped James fall into a deep sleep. He dreamed of his parents and his two sisters. It was a bright, sunny day, and they had gone to a beach to play catch. They laughed together, their faces lit up with joy. Somewhere, he heard waves crashing against rocks and seagulls crying overhead. To his annoyance, one seagull cried out again and again in a mournful way.

James looked up at the bird, but instead he saw a night sky with two bright moons and tree limbs reaching up to them. Puzzled, he turned to his father, but his father was gone. So were his mother and two sisters. Even the beach had vanished. He now stood alone in a forest.

"Am I back in Marus?" he asked.

Then he heard that mournful cry again. Was it an animal, or was it someone calling out? Either way, it sounded like a cry for help.

He went to investigate. Walking along an overgrown path, he was aware that his legs ached, as if he'd been walking a long time. The path was on an incline, going up and up.

Looking around, he noticed for the first time that the sides of the path were strewn with old baskets and boxes, with small, black rocks spilling out from their openings. James picked up one of the rocks. It looked and felt like coal.

I must be near a mine, he thought. He remembered that Deydra had mentioned mining as one of the industries here.

Suddenly the cry echoed through the woods again, somewhere up ahead. This time James could tell it was a young man's cry. James stopped and listened.

"Heeeeeeeelllllppppp!"

He dashed up the path. It angled around to the right and into a clearing littered with mining equipment. Besides the baskets and boxes, James also saw pickaxes, shovels, and upended wheelbarrows. Then, at the edge of the area, he saw a weather-beaten sign, hanging lopsided from a post, that said "Arinshill Mine."

James immediately assumed that the cry for help came from somewhere inside the mine on the other side of the clearing.

Someone is trapped, he thought. And he would have rushed forward if it hadn't been for a different, unexpected sound: an outburst of laughter. One man laughed alone, and then several joined in loudly and heartily.

Creeping from tree to tree, behind a wheelbarrow and then behind a large rock, James got a clearer view of what was happening. Near the entrance to the mine, several large and burly men, most with long hair and thick beards, were standing with torches held high. They wore short tunics, belted at the waist. Their legs were covered with breeches and knee-high boots. Through their legs, James could see that they circled a lumpy sack on the ground. Something inside the sack moved and wiggled.

"Heeeeeellllllpppp!" came a voice from the sack.

One of the men gave the sack a sharp kick. "Shut up," he growled.

"You're going to get into big trouble for this," the voice in the sack said, pained from the kick.

"Not as much trouble as you're in now," another man replied. Some of the men chuckled.

"I'll tell Father!"

"You won't be telling anybody anything," someone said and kicked him again.

"Let's take him into the cave," another man said.

"Wait," yet another barked, then knelt down and reached into the sack. His arm jerked around as whoever was inside twisted and resisted. "Stop it," the man demanded and punched the side of the sack.

"Sesta, what are you doing?" a younger member of the group asked.

"We don't want the ring to disappear with him, do we?" Sesta replied. "I'm going to take it off his finger."

The largest of the men, and probably the oldest since his hair was sprinkled with gray, put a hand on Sesta's shoulder. "Why?" he asked.

"Father gave it to him! It's valuable!"

"All the more reason why you should leave it," the large man said. "What will you do, wear it so that Father will see? He'll ask how you got it, and then we *will* be in trouble."

"I'll tell Father it was all we could find of him after he ran away."

"That makes no sense," the large man said firmly. "Why would he run away without the ring?"

Sesta stood up and complained, "You don't want me to have the ring, do you? You always were on *his* side. Even though he'll rob you of your rightful place as Father's heir, you'll stick up for him."

"I agree with Rastall," one of the others said.

Sesta then came up with another idea. "I know! We'll tell Father that he was killed by a wild animal and show the ring as proof!"

"This is a dirty business," Rastall said. "It will come back to haunt us one day."

"Not if we followed *my* plan."

Rastall stiffened his back, rising to his full height, a full head and shoulders over the others. "No! Imprisoning him in this cave is one thing, but killing him is another. I forbid it." He then added in a low, threatening tone, "Unless someone wants to challenge me."

The rest of the men shuffled their feet uneasily.

Sesta hooked a hand around the top of the sack. "Into the cave," he commanded.

Four of the men joined Sesta in picking up the sack, and then they all disappeared into the darkness. After a short while, they returned without the sack, most of their torches extinguished, and went their way silently into the dark forest.

James felt sick. The men must have thrown the man in the sack into a mine shaft. The one called Rastall wouldn't let them kill him, but what was the difference if they left him to die anyway?

James slipped out from behind the rock and, after making sure none of the men were on their way back, headed toward the cave. But as he approached the entrance, his feet seemed to sink in the dirt. Alarmed, he looked down at his shoes. They were covered with mud—up to his ankles now. He pulled with all his might, but he couldn't get free. Worse, he sank even farther. The mud was like quicksand. The more he struggled, the farther he descended into the brown goo. It was up to his knees, then his waist.

He gasped, the panic working through every pore of his body. He desperately looked for something to grab. The various mining tools were just out of reach. He called out for help, hoping now that the men *would* come back. Instead, a voice—the voice from the sack—echoed his call. "Help!" the two of them shouted.

The mud was now up to James's chest. Then his neck. His arms were useless. He closed his mouth tight as the wet dirt pressed on his lips. Snorting like a horse, he tried to keep the mud out of his nostrils. It was only a short matter of time before he would have to breathe in all the damp and dirt and death.

Then there were hands on him, pushing at him.

"Wake up, James," a soft voice said.

With a harsh, rattling intake of air, James rolled over. Fantya gazed down at him with a worried expression on her face.

"You were thrashing around under your covers," she said. "Are you all right?"

James nodded, still breathing as if he'd never taken a breath before. The sky was light gray from the rising sun. Fantya looked exactly as she had the night before: the same wide-eyed expression, the same clothes. She didn't look as if she hadn't been to sleep at all. James sat up and tried to shake the memory of the dream away.

"Bad dream?" she asked.

"Awful," he replied. "I saw a group of men put someone in an old mine, and when I went to help, I got stuck in quicksand."

Fantya patted his arm soothingly and assured him, "It was only a dream."

"But it seemed so real."

"There are a lot of mines around here, but I don't think you have to worry about quicksand." Fantya gave James's arm a gentle tug. "Come on. You have to get up now. We're ready to go to Dremat. We'll give you some breakfast on the way."

James then noticed that the horses were hitched up to the wagons. Once again, Visyn was busying himself by kicking dirt on a campfire.

Fantya said, "We're eager to get on with our business. And we will as soon as Nosz returns."

"Returns from where?"

She shrugged. "He said he had some business to take care of. Ah, here he comes now."

Nosz emerged from a path in the woods. "This isn't normal for us, but we're willing to oblige a regular customer," he was saying.

Then a man stepped out from behind Nosz. "You're wise," the man replied. "The biggest businesses are built on the backs of little favors."

The man was large and burly, with long hair and a thick beard. He wore a short tunic with a belt around the waist.

Underneath were dark breeches and black, knee-length boots. James had seen the man before—in his dream.

"Sesta!" James gasped.

Nosz looked up, annoyed at the impertinence of the boy. "How dare you call the master by his first name!" he demanded.

Sesta looked at James quizzically and asked, "Do I know you, boy?"

"No, sir," James said, unsure of what to say. "I mean, I ... I'm sorry."

"Mind your manners," Nosz growled. He and Sesta walked off toward Nosz's wagon.

"I thought you said you'd never been here before," Visyn said, approaching James from the dying embers of the campfire.

"I haven't."

"Then how do you know Sesta?" he asked.

"I don't know him. Who is he?"

"One of the many sons of Connam."

"Connam?" James asked, then remembered even while Visyn answered. Connam was the wealthiest and most powerful man in the southern part of Marus.

Visyn grunted and concluded, "He's very important to our trade. I hope you didn't offend him." Then he walked off.

"You still haven't answered how you know him," Fantya said.

James got to his feet. "He was one of the men in my dream. He wanted to kill whoever they'd kidnapped."

"But you've never seen him before. How is it that you dreamed about him?"

"Good question," James said.

Fantya narrowed her eyes, as if she were working out a difficult math problem. "But if *he's* real, do you think maybe your dream was real?" she asked.

James shivered. "That's not possible. Dreams aren't real."

"And yet, there stands the man from your dream." She gestured toward Nosz and Sesta. They stood next to Nosz's wagon. The two men shook hands, and Sesta disappeared into the forest. "What else do you remember from your dream?"

James recounted everything. Afterward, Fantya said, "You saw a sign that said 'Arinshill Mine'?"

"Yes."

"There is an Arinshill Mine not far from here. I have seen signs for it when I have walked alone in the woods."

Not always alone, James thought as he remembered hearing her shout angrily at Nosz—and the sound of the slap.

"Let's go," Fantya eagerly said.

"Go?"

Without waiting for him, she headed briskly for the path into the forest. "To the mine," she said over her shoulder.

James raced after her. "But it was only a dream," he reminded her.

She went on anyway.

"Where are you going?" Visyn shouted at them.

"We'll be back!" Fantya called without slowing down.

Visyn let loose a stream of words that James assumed was the Palatian version of swearing.

CHAPTER FOUR

◆———◆

The sign said "Arinshill Mine" and was broken and tilted exactly as James had seen it in his dream. "This is nuts," James whispered.

He and Fantya walked into the clearing. Everything in the dream was there: the mining equipment, the baskets and boxes, the pickaxes and shovels and upended wheelbarrows, all cluttered with bits of coal and soot. And on the opposite side of the clearing was the mouth of the cave.

"Is this what you dreamed?" she asked him.

He wanted to lie. He wanted to say it was nothing like his dream so they could turn around and go back. His skin started to go goose-pimply. This wasn't normal, to have dreams become real.

"Well?" she prodded him.

"Yes, it is," he finally admitted.

Fantya went to the cave and jumped up and down on the dry dirt. "No quicksand."

James was slightly relieved. "That means my dream wasn't completely right. Maybe there isn't anyone in the cave either."

"There's only one way to find out." Fantya cupped her hands around the sides of her mouth and shouted, "Hello! Is anyone in there?"

"Heeeeellllllppp!" came a voice from the darkness.

James felt his skin crawl. It was the same voice he'd heard in his dream.

Fantya ventured into the cave but stopped at the edge of the shadows. Careful to avoid the area where he'd sunk in the mud in his dream, James also entered the cave.

"We won't get very far without a torch," James said.

Fantya looked around the ground. "The men in your dream went in."

"They had torches."

"Maybe they left one behind."

"Heeeeelllppp!" came the voice again.

"We're coming!" Fantya shouted impatiently as she picked up an old oil lamp. It was fractured and dry. She dropped it again.

James went to the far side of the cave opening. He imagined one of the men casually tossing his extinguished torch to one side as they came out. Sure enough, he saw a long, slender stick of wood with a ball of cloth and tar on its end.

"Here," James called out, picking up the torch.

Fantya smiled. "Well done." She tucked her hand into a pocket and produced a small book of matches. In an instant, the match was lit and so was the torch. Made braver by the light, the two of them crept farther into the cave.

Similar to the clearing outside, the inside of the cave was a mess of old mining materials. They stepped over and around more wheelbarrows and pickaxes, past a wooden shack, and over holes in the ground. Timber that had once braced the walls and ceiling now lay rotting across the floor.

"Heeeeelllllppp!" the voice called.

Fantya called back, "Keep shouting so we'll know if we're getting close."

"What do you want me to shout?" the voice asked.

"Anything!" Fantya replied, exasperated.

The voice began to count loudly. "One, two, three, four ..."

James guessed that the voice belonged to a boy not much older than himself and likely a few years younger than Fantya—possibly 15 or 16.

The voice had reached the number 28 when James and Fantya found the edge of the mine shaft he'd been thrown into. They held the torch over the side and peered down. The shaft itself was unfinished, going down only about 30 feet below them. If there'd once been a ladder on the side of the unfinished shaft, it was long gone. A teenage boy lay at the bottom.

"Hello," he said cordially, blinking up at them.

"Hi," James responded with a slight wave.

"How are we going to get him out?" Fantya asked.

"I don't know."

"Rope?" the boy called up to them. "The miners used hoists to haul out the buckets of coal. Look for a hoist and you'll find the rope attached."

James and Fantya shrugged at each other and obeyed. Within minutes, they'd found a hoist with a rope long enough to drop down to the boy.

"You grab the rope and we'll pull you up," James told him.

"I'm afraid I can't."

"Why not?"

"My hands are tied. So are my feet."

Fantya looked at James skeptically and announced, "I'm not pulling you both up."

"We'll have to pull ourselves up," James replied. He grabbed the end of the rope and tied it to the largest of the nearby support beams. He then went to the edge of the shaft, dropped the rope into the hole, and began to climb down.

"Be careful," Fantya said.

James held the rope with both hands and braced his feet against the side of the shaft, just like the photos of mountain climbers he'd once seen. But James was no mountain climber, and he found his feet slipping away, which slammed his whole body against the wall. This happened several times as he descended the shaft. By the time he reached the bottom, he was banged up and shaken.

The teenager now sat helplessly against the wall. He was surprisingly gangly, with long arms and legs, a thin neck, and a face James could hardly make out in the darkness. He had a mop on his head that looked more like tumbleweed than hair.

"I knew you would come," the young man said with a smile.

James was perplexed. "What?" he asked.

"I saw you in my dream last night."

"You saw *me?*"

"You hid behind a big rock. You saw what they did to me. You were going to come and help me, but ..."

"But what?"

"But you couldn't. I don't know why."

"I couldn't help you because I *woke up*," James said, his skin starting to crawl again. "I wasn't really behind the rock. I only *dreamed* I was behind the rock."

"Then why did I see you in my dream? How did I know you saw what happened?"

"I didn't *see* what happened. I only *dreamed* I saw it."

The young man's mouth fell open. "That means that you dreamed my experience. And I dreamed your dream."

"Are you going to chat in that hole all day or are you coming back up?" Fantya asked.

"Can you stand up?" James asked the boy.

"They bound me around the ankles. Unfortunately, I've lost all the feeling in my feet and hands."

"Roll over a little while I try to untie your hands," James said. The teenager turned to his side. James pondered the leather straps on his wrists, then began to pick at them. "They sure didn't want to take any chances with you," he said between grunts.

"They're my brothers," the boy said sadly. "I don't know what got into them."

"Run-of-the-mill hatred is what I figure," James said, then groaned. The knots tore at his fingers as he tore at the knots.

"My name is Glennall," the teen said.

"Nice to meet you. I'm James."

Fantya shouted, "This torch isn't going to last much longer."

"I'm doing the best I can," James called back. It took several minutes, but he finally undid the straps.

"Much better," Glennall said. He waved his hands in the air. "But they're dead for the time being. I don't think I'll be able to grab the rope to climb out."

"Rub them," James suggested.

Glennall tried. The effect was like rubbing two packs of sausages together.

"Let me," James offered, clasping Glennall's hands in his own.

Something happened then that startled him. In a flash, James saw a picture in his mind. He stood in the front hall of a mansion. Glennall stood next to him. They were both scrubbed clean, their hair combed, and they were dressed in silver coats and breeches, with white lace shirts. A heavyset man with a round, jowly face and silver hair pulled back in a ponytail smiled at them. James had the immediate impression they were being praised for something by the heavyset man. He felt comfortable and satisfied, as if his life was the best it had ever been. Then the picture disappeared.

Glennall had let go of James's hands and was staring at him with an expression of shock.

"What was *that?*" James asked.

"I haven't the slightest idea," Glennall replied. "I wonder who that man was?"

"I've never seen him before," James said, then stopped cold. He suddenly realized what Glennall had just said. "What man?" he asked warily.

"The man in the dream."

"What dream?"

"The dream we just had. You and I were standing in the front hall of some sort of palace. A rather rotund man was complimenting us for something."

James felt weak in the knees. "But that means we had the exact same dream."

"Only in a manner of speaking," remarked Glennall. "I think we saw *two halves* of the same dream. My dream was from *my* point of view. I assume your dream was from *your* point of view. The same as the dreams we both had last night."

"But that's not possible."

"Possible or not, it happened."

Fantya called down, "We're going to lose our light if you don't make haste!"

"We'll figure it out when I get your feet untied," James said as he attacked the straps on Glennall's feet. They were just as difficult to untie as the straps on his wrists had been. But a few minutes later, Glennall was free from his bonds.

Glennall tried to flex his muscles. "My hands and feet are useless," he said. "How am I going to get up?"

"We'll have to tie the rope around your chest. Then Fantya and I will pull you up."

James looped the rope around Glennall's torso. After making sure it was tied securely, he shimmied up the rope to the top. This was a painful task since his fingers were raw from untying the leather straps, and his legs were tired from so much unusual exertion. He was red-faced and exhausted by the time he saw Fantya again.

She hadn't exaggerated. The torch was beginning to lose its flame. "I don't want to be trapped in here in the dark," she said. She looked worried.

"All right. Let's hurry and pull him up," James responded.

Fantya hooked the torch into a circle of iron that had been mounted on the side of the cave to hold an oil lamp. She came back to James, and together they grabbed the rope and began to pull. Glennall wasn't heavy, but his clothes and limbs caught against the side of the mine shaft. He "oofed" and "ouched" the entire way up.

"I hope his father is rich and will give us a very large reward," Fantya puffed.

"If he's who I think he is," James said, "his father is the richest man around."

The torch flickered as if to threaten them. James and Fantya quickly lifted Glennall out of the mine shaft. "My feet and hands are pins and needles," Glennall complained. As a result, James and Fantya had to carry him through the tunnel.

The torch gave up its light just as the mouth of the cave came into view.

"By the grace of the Unseen One," Glennall whispered.

"Are you a believer in the Unseen One?" Fantya asked.

"Of course," Glennall replied, as if *not* believing was an absurd thought.

Fantya seemed mystified. "I've never met anyone who believed."

They reached the clearing and winced at the sunlight.

"Thank you, Fantya," a deep voice boomed. "You've saved me from the trouble."

CHAPTER FIVE

James knew who it was even before he shielded his eyes to see more clearly. Nosz stood before them with two broad-shouldered men of olive complexion and the look of street thugs. One had a puckered scar disfiguring his cheek.

"Saved you from *what* trouble, Nosz?" Fantya asked.

"The trouble of getting the boy out of the mine shaft myself."

"What do you want with him?" she demanded.

"Strictly business, my dear."

"What kind of business? I am returning to my father," said Glennall as resolutely as he could manage. His face was screwed up against the sunlight. He looked pale and haggard. Red spots of acne dotted his forehead and nose. One of his eyes was black, probably from being kicked by his brothers. "I'm the son of Connam, and you will stand aside!"

Nosz was undaunted. "You're coming with me," he insisted. "It's been arranged with your brothers."

"My brothers will have no say over me once I've spoken with my father."

"Which is why you'll never speak to your father again. You're coming with me to Palatia."

"Palatia! I have no business in Palatia."

"You will once I've *sold* you." Nosz said it in such a casual way that James almost didn't catch it.

Fantya did, and she stepped forward angrily. "We don't deal in slaves," she said through gritted teeth. "My father will never allow it."

"Your father and I have severed our partnership, Fantya," said Nosz. "He will go his way, and I will go mine. *I warned you*."

"We'll be the better for it."

"Perhaps you will. But in the meantime, I have negotiated a lucrative business deal with the sons of Connam. In no time at all, I will be a very wealthy man, while you and your family continue as second-rate traders. I hope you enjoy your life."

"What does this have to do with me?" Glennall demanded.

"You're part of the arrangement," Nosz explained. "I'm doing your brothers a favor by getting rid of you for them." Nosz signaled the two thugs. "Take him."

The two goons made for Glennall. He tried to run, but his legs were in no condition to carry him very far. The men grabbed him easily.

James put up a fight until one of the thugs backhanded him with a fist. Stunned, he fell to the ground. He was quickly seized and bound.

Fantya also fought, going straight at Nosz with her finger-nails extended like a lioness's claws.

Nosz caught hold of her wrist. "Be careful, girl, or I'll take you with us," he threatened.

"You wouldn't dare."

He smiled cruelly, twisting her wrist until she squirmed from the pain. "Go back to your father," he commanded. "And if you know what's good for you, you won't say a word about this to anyone. Speak of it and you'll be stirring up trouble for yourself with the sons of Connam. Believe me, you'll hurt no one but your family."

"I hate you."

Grabbing her face, he kissed her roughly on the lips. Then he pushed her away.

She stumbled back a few steps, wiped her mouth, and spat, "You're a pig."

Nosz glared at her. His face went red, and he raised his fists as if he might explode into great violence. Instead, he jerked his head at his two thugs. They pulled James and Glennall to their feet.

Fantya suddenly realized what they were doing. "Why are you taking James?" she asked.

"Because there's nothing to stop *him* from trying to reach Connam with news about his missing son."

"You have no right!" Fantya insisted. "He's a stranger here. He has nothing to do with any of us!"

"He does now."

"What if I don't want to come with you?" James said. "What if I shout long and hard that I've been kidnapped?"

"Then I'll kill you here and now," Nosz answered, and James knew he meant it. "You have no choice, boy. Your life is forfeit to me now."

"But ... you can't sell *me* as a slave."

Again the cruel smile spread across Nosz's face.

James and Glennall sat on the floor in the back of Nosz's wagon, feeling every jerk and bump as the wheels hit rocks or dipped into ruts in the road. Unlike Deydra's wagon, which seemed like a home on wheels, this wagon was little better than a barn with a bed. A cot stretched along one wall, and an unlit oil lamp swung from a hook above. The rest of the space was taken up with crates of goods, straw and dirt on the floor, a trunk of clothes, and a rusty, potbellied stove.

Chained to a ring in the wall, James and Glennall sat in

near darkness. What little light there was came through the gaps between the slats of wood. The shutters on the two small windows were closed and clamped down.

"He won't get away with this, you know," Glennall said.

"He's doing pretty well so far," James replied.

They had left the mountain an hour or two before, circled around the bustling city of Dremat, and continued southwest on the main road to Palatia. Nosz and his two henchmen were in the front, driving the horse. Apart from the occasional noise of other passing horses, wagons, and people hailing from the side of the road, nothing else could be heard.

After a while, Glennall said, "I suppose you're wondering how I got in this mess."

"The question crossed my mind," James acknowledged.

"My brothers are jealous of me."

James glanced at the red acne spots on Glennall's face, his patch of wild hair, and his gangly frame. He compared it to the strong, rugged, handsome men at the cave. "They're jealous of you?" he asked skeptically.

"It's not so hard to believe," Glennall said defensively. "I'm my father's favorite."

James looked at him doubtfully.

"You don't believe me."

James shrugged.

"You don't seem to understand. Rastall, Sesta, Turnan, Drouse, Naud, and Yon are my father's sons by Agula, his first wife. He adopted Cannap, Fortawince, Selsond, and Pa'an."

The names meant nothing to James.

Glennall continued, a hint of pride in his voice. "But my younger brother, Transe, and I are the sons of the woman he loved the most: Elega."

"So?"

"So my father has a special affection for me and Transe. Me, particularly, because I am the oldest son of Elega."

"Where's your mother now?"

"She died giving birth to Transe."

"Oh. That's too bad."

Glennall looked thoughtful. "I think that's another reason my father is so protective with me and Transe."

James rattled their chains. "It looks like his protection hasn't helped much."

"The point is, my father has always treated me differently. More so after the visions began."

"Visions?"

"They started when I came down with a fever back when I was a small boy. I have these terrible headaches, blinding in their pain, that leave me weak and delirious."

"That's tough."

"I suppose so," said Glennall indifferently. "Because of them, my father has made me stay at home."

"So you didn't get out much."

"No, but I was allowed to read my father's entire library and every other book I could get my hands on. I'm surprisingly intelligent for my age." Glennall smiled.

James prodded him on. "You were telling me about your visions."

"Once," he began again, "I rose from my sickbed and announced that one of our mines had collapsed and many men had died. My family assured me that no mine had collapsed— I'd only had a nightmare. I said that one would. Unfortunately, I didn't know which mine or when it would happen. My father and brothers said they couldn't close down the mines while we waited around for my disaster to happen, so they did nothing. Two days later, a mine collapsed and killed 54 men."

"It might've been a coincidence."

Glennall continued, "And there was another time when I saw a vision in which men at one of our timber camps were hurt by a falling tree. Once again, I didn't know where it would happen or when. So no one heeded me. Sadly, a tree fell, breaking the bones of several men who couldn't get out of the way in time. One died."

"But why would your visions make your brothers jealous?" James asked.

"Those didn't. But the ones I had later did."

"Why?"

"Because the visions were about them."

James looked at Glennall curiously.

Glennall explained, "I had one in which my brothers were starving. They gathered around me, begging for food. I gave them as much as they needed and saved their lives."

"You had them eating out of the palm of your hand."

"That's right."

"And you told them about the vision."

"Why wouldn't I?"

James rolled his eyes. "You may be intelligent for your age, but you're not very smart."

"What do you mean?"

"Didn't it occur to you that telling them was a stupid idea?"

"Why? It was what happened in my vision."

"Because they'd resent you," James growled. "It might even make them want to hurt you."

"Oh, I see what you mean," Glennall said as if the thought hadn't occurred to him before. "I assumed they would be happy for me to save their lives."

"Maybe they will be if it ever actually happens. But not now. They're your *older* brothers. Older brothers don't like to be in debt to their younger brothers."

"Why not?"

James tried to think of a good answer but couldn't. "I don't know. That's just how it is. I've got two younger sisters, and one of them is a real goody-two-shoes. She was always getting me in trouble."

"How?"

"Telling on me when I did something wrong."

Glennall suddenly frowned. "Oh."

"Did you tell on your brothers?"

"Only because my father asked me to."

"Oh, brother," James said with a sigh.

"Last year he said I could get out of the house to be his personal messenger. He sent me to the various work sites to give messages to my brothers. He also said to report to him if they weren't doing their work properly."

"And you did."

"Of course I did. I couldn't lie to my father."

James shook his head disparagingly. "And you wonder why they threw you in the cave?"

"It's not my fault," Glennall complained. "I was only doing what my father asked. My brothers had all gone off together to our home near Dremat to discuss their various responsibilities around my father's lands. At least, that's what they were *supposed* to be doing. My father was too ill to attend, so he sent me to represent him."

"He asked *you* to speak for him?"

"Yes. He gave me his ceremonial gown and his ring and said to advise them."

"In other words, he made you the Big Cheese over your brothers," said James. "That's a recipe for disaster. So what happened?"

"When I went to find them, they weren't there. A servant said they'd gone to Dremat. I couldn't think why, so I searched for them and found them feasting in the city."

"You mean they were off having fun when they should have been working?"

"Yes."

"So you confronted them."

"I told them Father would be *very* displeased if he knew they had gone to Dremat when they were supposed to be discussing family business."

James held up his hand. "Don't tell me, let me guess: That's when they hauled you up to the mine."

"Yes."

"What a surprise."

"They put me in a sack and carried me up to the cave. They hit me and kicked me and … and some of them even spoke of … of … killing me." He lowered his head into his folded arms. James thought he'd begun to cry.

James waited.

"Rastall was the only one to defend me," Glennall eventually said. "He told them not to kill me for fear that it might come back as a curse upon them. He said to sell me as a slave instead."

"What a pal."

Glennall was quiet for a moment, then added, "Dilliam said it would be like this."

"Who's Dilliam?"

"A wise man who lives in a shelter near our home. Some call him a priest. He said that the hand of the Unseen One was upon me. My father was worried about that. He said those who are chosen by the Unseen One get nothing but trouble. But Dilliam said it wasn't my father's choice, though he admitted I would be ridiculed and abused."

"I don't know anything about the Unseen One. But I know you *will* be ridiculed and abused if you act like a turnip head."

"Turnip head!" Glennall was indignant.

"Sure," James replied. "Marching around like a little king, telling on your brothers, having visions about being better than they are ... What do you expect?"

"It's not my fault and it's not fair," Glennall sniffed. "I only hope the Unseen One will make things right and grant me the means for revenge. One day I'll pay them back."

"Fat chance," James said.

"I believe He will." He looked at James hopefully. "Especially now that you're here."

"What do you mean?"

"The Unseen One is at work in you somehow."

"What are you talking about?" James said, annoyed.

"You have eyes of different colors—the mark of the Unseen One."

"I don't believe all that stuff."

"You don't believe?" Glennall asked. "But your eyes are different colors." He said it as if that fact meant James had to be a believer.

"That's some kind of accident. A doctor could explain it."

"What about your dreams and what happened to us in the mine shaft?"

"They were just dreams, that's all," James said. "A coincidence. It's not like every dream I have comes true. When I dreamed about you, I also dreamed I was on a beach with my family. Did that happen? No. And after I dreamed about you, I thought I was being swallowed up in quicksand. Did that happen? No."

"Not all dreams are dreams that come true. But there are dreams *within* dreams—"

"Listen to me," James said as he turned to face him angrily. "I don't know anything about your Unseen One. And I can't explain how these crazy dreams happened. But I don't believe in all this mumbo-jumbo about visions."

"But you *have* to believe."

"I don't have to do anything," snapped James. "Look, I don't even belong here!"

"Then where do you belong?"

The question stopped James. He didn't know where he belonged anymore. In Odyssey with Aunt Edna? In some other part of the country with his two sisters? He felt all alone.

The wagon suddenly stopped as Nosz shouted, "Whoa!"

After a few minutes, the door to the back of the wagon was yanked open. Light poured in, causing the boys to blink. The henchman with the scar on his cheek climbed in. He kicked at them to get out of the way while he unlocked their chains.

"Get out," he grunted. "And don't do anything you'll regret."

CHAPTER SIX

—◆————————◆—

James and Glennall climbed out of the wagon. Nosz had stopped on the side of the road. A wide, treeless field spread out beside them. James was startled again by the colors: the richness of the green grass, the depth of blue in the sky, even the darkness of the brown coats on several saddled horses nearby. He wondered if everything seemed brighter because he'd been in the dark wagon—or if this was something peculiar about Marus. He suspected it was Marus.

Next to the horses sat several men wearing uniforms unlike any James had ever seen. Their coats were gray with gold buttons and extended to their midcalves. Underneath they wore crisp, white shirts, wool vests, and gray breeches to match the coats. Their boots were a shiny black. The men looked as if they'd been riding and had stopped to rest.

Nosz approached the two boys and quickly dusted the dirt off them with his palm. "Straighten up," he said in a low voice. "Look presentable."

One of the men in uniform, thin and balding, approached. He munched on an apple, then threw away the core. "What do you have this time, Nosz?" he asked.

"Well, Valad, for you …" Nosz began as he hitched up his trousers. He elbowed James to get him to stand straighter. "I have two clever and resourceful house servants, sir."

"I said I wanted to bring a present from Marus for my master," Valad said. "I said nothing about slaves."

"What better present than two house servants from Marus? You know what good workers Marutians make."

The balding man circled James and Glennall, eyeing them from head to foot. "They look like a couple of scamps to me," he said skeptically.

"Beat them regularly and you'll see how hard they work."

"Lay a hand on me and you'll answer to my father," Glennall challenged.

"Shut up," Nosz ordered as he backhanded him.

Glennall would have fallen to his knees if James hadn't grabbed his arm to help steady him.

"Who's your father, boy?" the man asked.

Nosz nervously interrupted. "The boy is—"

"I wasn't asking you, Nosz," Valad said sharply. He looked at Glennall closely. "Who is your father that I should be afraid of him?"

Glennall rubbed his stung cheek. "He is Connam, the owner of all the lands east of here," he offered boldly.

"I know of Connam," the man said.

"Then you know how powerful he is," said Glennall.

"Indeed I do. I have also seen many of his sons at the auctions in Dremat." A wiry smile crept across the man's face. "And I cannot believe that Connam—or his robust sons— would have a squirt like you for a relative."

The other uniformed men laughed.

Nosz looked relieved. "This boy has a wild imagination," he said.

"I promise you: Connam is my father," Glennall insisted.

"Show me proof," Valad said.

"Take me back to Dremat and I will show you proof."

"We won't be going all the way back to Dremat to indulge your fantasies," Nosz growled.

"What about you?" Valad asked James. "Do you also have a powerful father?"

"My father is dead," James replied icily.

"And you have no inheritance? No home?"

James lowered his head. "No." Then he added, "But that doesn't make me a slave."

"As good as one now," the man said. He gestured to Nosz. "Deliver them to my master's house with my compliments. If nothing else, he'll enjoy their Marutian spunk."

"And payment?"

"I will pay you when they've been delivered in good order," Valad said.

The deal completed, one of Nosz's thugs herded James and Glennall back into the wagon, chained their arms, and closed them in. A couple of minutes later, they were bouncing down the road again.

"What will happen to us now?" James wondered aloud.

Glennall shook his head. "I don't trust that Valad character. Did you recognize his uniform?"

"No."

"He's a member of King Akvych's security force."

"I don't know who King Akvych is."

"He is the king of Palatia," Glennall answered with a quizzical look. "And his security force includes some of the most ruthless and disreputable men alive. They occasionally venture into Marus to cause trouble."

"You mean they raid the towns and villages?"

"No. They try to spread dissension among the people who work for the landowners. My father has had to chase them off many times. If the Palatians can get our workers to rebel against the landowners, they'll have an excuse to invade. They'd love nothing more than to get their hands on our country and make us all slaves. That's the kind of people they are."

James thought about this for a moment. "And we've been sold to the master of one of them?"

"So it would seem."

James slid onto his back, rested his chained arms on his chest, and said hopelessly, "Great. It gives me something to look forward to."

Glennall sat quietly for a moment, then said, "I was wondering what would happen if we grabbed hands again, like we did in the cave. The Unseen One may reveal something to us."

"I told you already: I don't believe in that."

"Then there's no harm in trying."

"Why do you need me? You had dreams and visions before I came along."

Glennall responded, "I've been thinking about that. Suppose my dreams and visions were only partly complete. I only saw part of what I needed to see. Just like I only saw part of what happened at the cave, and you saw the other part."

"Sounds like double-talk to me."

"Perhaps when we touch hands, we may see everything we need to see completely."

"Perhaps?" James said, his voice rising over the sound of the wagon wheels on the dirt. "There is no *perhaps*. This isn't possible, do you understand? None of it is."

"Then how do you explain it?"

"I can't explain it," James replied stubbornly. "And I don't have to."

Glennall reached out his hands, stretching to their limit. "Take my hands."

James looked at them without moving. "It's crazy."

"So you keep saying. Take them anyway."

"I don't like it. It gives me the creeps."

"You may as well try. I won't leave you alone until you do."

James looked from Glennall's hands to his face and back again. On impulse, he grabbed Glennall's hands in his.

The two boys tensed as they looked at each other. The chains rattled. A horse snorted. The wagon moved on relentlessly.

"Nothing happened," James observed. "See?"

Glennall shook his head. "That doesn't mean anything," he maintained.

"Nothing happened—that's what it means."

"The Unseen One does as *He* wills, not as we might wish."

James sat back. He was relieved, but strangely disappointed.

It took three days to reach Muirk, the capital city of Palatia, as Nosz stopped frequently to sell goods and take orders for future deliveries. Except for those brief moments when they were allowed out to relieve themselves, the two boys remained in the back of the wagon the entire time. But that didn't stop them from peeking through the slats in the wagon walls.

The buildings in the city weren't tall—at least, not like the skyscrapers James knew—but they were still impressive with their lavish brickwork, broad columns, and white pillars. Occasionally James saw what looked liked statues and pyramid-shaped monuments. People shouted, hawkers sold wares from makeshift stalls, vendors offered their best deals, pedestrians dodged between horses, and beggars appealed for alms.

Eventually the traffic and people thinned out as Nosz drove to the outskirts of the city. They passed high walls and wrought-iron gates, behind which sat large mansions.

Nosz slowed at the gate of one such mansion. A guard dressed in a uniform identical to those of Valad and his men checked on Nosz's purpose for being there, then opened the gates to let them through. They traveled down a long driveway, past enormous oaks, and then skirted to the left around the front entrance of the mansion.

They pulled up to a rear entrance, obviously used by the servants. Nosz brought the wagon to a stop. The scar-faced henchman opened the door, undid the boys' chains, and pushed them out. James stretched long and hard.

A middle-aged man with long, brown hair, bushy side whiskers, and the posture and shape of a long plank of wood appeared at the back door. He wore a silver jacket over his shirt and breeches—the same kind of jacket James had seen in his dream. The two boys exchanged looks.

The man seemed to recognize Nosz and greeted him formally, and the two men went inside. A couple of minutes later, they returned. Chatting amiably, Nosz signaled his two pals to get back onto the wagon. Then he hesitated near the boys as if he might say something to them, but he merely grunted and walked past.

"I won't forget you, Nosz," Glennall said.

Nosz didn't reply but climbed up onto the driver's bench, barked at the horse to get moving, and drove away.

James had a wild thought about trying to run for it. He considered the vast estate, the many places there must be to hide, and the possibilities a city like Muirk might hold for him. It didn't look as though he'd ever figure out how to get back to his own world anyway, so why not make the best of it?

Glennall watched him as if he knew what James was thinking. He slowly, almost imperceptibly, shook his head.

"So you're a gift to my master," the man with the sideburns said. "How thoughtful of Valad."

"Where exactly are we?" James asked.

The man with the sideburns quickly struck him across the

face. It didn't hurt as much as it startled. "Speak only when you're spoken to," the man commanded. "That's the first rule in this house."

"Yes, sir," James said, rubbing his cheek.

"My name is Tezst, and you two will answer to me," the man said, tucking his thumbs into his waistcoat. It was silver, like the jacket. "It doesn't matter what anyone else tells you, *I* have the final word. Apart from the master, of course. But you probably won't see him much. He's a very busy man. And he likes the servants to be invisible. Do you understand?"

"Yes, sir," James and Glennall muttered.

"He and his wife are away on the king's business for a couple of weeks, which will give us ample time to train you properly. You will work hard, *very* hard. Your lives are not your own. You live to serve the master now."

James raised his hand, not daring to speak again without permission.

Tezst looked as James's hand as if he didn't understand why it was raised. "What are you doing?" he demanded.

"I need to ask a question."

"Permission to ask is granted."

"Exactly *who* is the master?"

Tezst looked at James open-mouthed. "You don't know?"

"No, sir."

"He is the head of the king's security forces. His name is Alexx, but you will never call him by name. Now come inside. I will show you your sleeping quarters, arrange to have you bathed and given suitable outfits"—at this he gave James a disapproving look—"and then introduce you to your responsibilities."

CHAPTER SEVEN

Their "quarters" were two small, windowless rooms near the kitchen with bare wooden floors and shelves of supplies on the walls. Each room had a cot, a stand with an oil lamp, and a trunk for any belongings they might have.

"Don't worry about heat," Tezst said. "You'll get plenty of that from the kitchen."

Much to James's embarrassment, they were then taken back to the kitchen, where they were forced to strip, get into a large tub of cool water, and given a hard scrub by an old woman named Ruislip. Glennall didn't seem to mind at all, as if he were used to it.

Tezst measured James and Glennall for their servant's uniforms, then sent Cowen, another slave, to the city to fetch them from the tailor. Cowen returned with the clothes a couple of hours later and helped the boys dress properly.

A stooped and bald old man, Cowen shuffled around Glennall and James, muttering as he helped them put on the white shirts and gray breeches, which buttoned to a pair of long, thin stockings, which in turn went into black leather shoes. The outfits were then topped with matching gray waistcoats.

"Now let me look at you," Cowen said. The old man inspected them, starting with their feet, then slowly raising his eyes, adjusting a button here or picking off lint there, and finally, for the first time, looking full in their faces. "You seem familiar to me," he said to Glennall. He then turned his attention to James. When they made eye contact, Cowen suddenly jerked his head back as if someone had slapped him in the face.

"What's wrong?" James asked.

"Nothing," the old man said. But his voice was full of *something*. He glanced back at James's face as if to confirm what he'd seen, then said, "Now follow me and I will explain your responsibilities."

They were told that their day would begin with chopping wood for the many fireplaces around the house and then distributing it to the 16 bedrooms upstairs and the eight rooms downstairs.

After the wood was taken care of, they would help Ruislip and her assistants to prepare and serve the meals. Then they were to clean the dishes. In between the various meals, they were to help the other house servants clean the rooms, dust the furniture, wash and wax the floors, polish silver, and, in the evenings, see that the lamps were lit throughout the house.

Other than that, they were at the beck and call of whoever needed them.

"This is worse than living at Aunt Edna's," James whispered to Glennall at one point.

Cowen explained that, as house servants, they were to be nearly invisible. "You may be seen, but never noticed," he said. "Never draw attention to yourselves. And never appear as if your work is hard. The master wants us to look dignified at all times. That's why he dresses us better than most slaves."

Their first morning of work came quicker than the two young men would have liked. It was still dark, and the early spring dew chilled them. But they were soon hot and sweaty from chopping wood. This was made worse by the overwhelming heat from the two brick ovens in the kitchen, which Ruislip kept lit most of the day. By the end of breakfast, James thought that every muscle in his body had gone stiff.

James noticed that Glennall didn't groan or complain.

Instead, he kept a fixed smile on his face the entire time he worked. "Aren't you stiff and sore?" James asked.

Glennall nodded.

"But you don't show it."

Glennall's smile was cold and humorless. He answered through gritted teeth, "We're never to make our work look hard, remember? Besides, I'm practicing for my brothers."

"Your brothers?"

"I never want them to see my pain," he replied. "I will bear what I must with a smile. I will suffer whatever I must suffer secretly. I will store it in my heart and relish it until the day when I see my brothers again."

"And then what?"

"Then I will smile while the Unseen One makes things right."

True to Glennall's resolve, James never heard him complain.

By the evening of the first day, all James could do was lie in bed and moan. Later, however, Cowen brought him a bottle filled with a thick, yellow liquid. "Rub this into your muscles and you'll feel better by morning," Cowen said.

"What is it?" James asked.

"An ointment from our country."

"*Our* country?"

"Marus," Cowen replied. "I heard that you and the young man are from Marus. I am from Marus as well."

"I'm not from Marus," James said as he began to put the ointment on his legs. Almost immediately, he felt a soothing warmth sink deep into his aches. He felt better.

"I misheard, then."

"Not really. I was *brought* from Marus. But I'm really from …" He hesitated, not sure of how to answer. "I'm from somewhere else."

Cowen leaned forward and said quietly, "I know where you are from."

"You do?" James whispered back.

Cowen nodded. "You are wise to keep your mouth shut. At least until we know what's to be done."

"Huh?"

Cowen put a finger to his lips and stood up. "Use the ointment sparingly," he said. "There isn't much." Then he left the room.

Long after Cowen had left and he was supposed to be asleep, James pondered their conversation. Could it be that Cowen was from *his* world?

Over the next few days, James looked for an opportunity to talk to Cowen again, but Cowen seemed to avoid James at every turn. Even Glennall noticed it.

"Did you say something to offend him?" Glennall asked James.

James told Glennall about the odd conversation they'd had.

Glennall was excited to hear it. "Why didn't you tell me right away?" he asked.

"Because you make such a big deal out of everything and start yapping about the Unseen One and all that nonsense."

Glennall frowned. "That's no reason to keep secrets from me. Don't you see? Our paths have joined. We're on the same road together, linked for some hidden purpose. So we mustn't keep any secrets from each other."

James merely grunted. It was exactly what he figured Glennall would say.

"Another Marutian!" Glennall went on. "Wonderful! Perhaps the Unseen One has brought us together to plan an escape!"

"Don't be such a chowderhead," James said. "It's a *coincidence,* that's all." But in his heart, James wondered if Cowen might know how to get him back to his own world.

A couple of days later, James and Glennall were assigned to clean the downstairs rooms. They began with the two modest drawing rooms. Then they moved on to the larger banquet hall. Next they worked in the smaller dining room, which was used for informal meals. From there they cleaned the master's "meeting" room. The master also had a library and a separate room for games, such as billiards, darts, and table tennis.

The last room they cleaned was the master's study. For James, it was the most impressive—a large, richly furnished room dominated by an enormous stone fireplace with columns on each side and sculpted patterns of diamonds along the top. A coat of arms took up most of the overmantel. Fitted bookcases stretched out from both sides of the fireplace. Large, framed paintings of great Palatian battles with Palatian soldiers vanquishing all enemies adorned the walls. The master's desk, made of dark oak, sat in the center on a woven carpet filled with geometric designs of red, black, and gold.

James was awed by the room. Glennall shrugged it off. "My father's study is better than this," he said and wandered to the desk. He nonchalantly picked up the stacks of papers and opened a large ledger that sat on the side.

"What are you doing?" James asked.

Glennall pulled out a rag that had been tucked in his back pocket. "I'm wiping the dust from the furniture, as we were told." He sat down in the chair and absentmindedly rubbed the rag around while he studied the papers and ledger.

"But you're not supposed to *look* at the master's things."

Glennall chuckled. "There are a lot of negative numbers in this ledger."

"It's none of your business."

"The master is spending more than he's earning."

"Get away from there."

"Part of the problem is that he's investing heavily in King Akvych's mines in the west. Everyone knows they're petering out. They reached their peak years ago."

"If he wants to go broke, let him go broke."

"And then what? He'll have to sell us. If I have to be a slave, I'd rather be a slave in a rich man's house than in some hovel or on a ship."

"But—"

Glennall picked up a quill pen, dipped it in the inkwell, and started to write.

"Are you nuts?" James whispered, keeping a panicked eye on the door.

"I'm writing a note to the master. It will help him."

"Maybe he doesn't want your help."

"He'll want this help," Glennall replied. "I'm telling him something that no one outside my family knows—that we have just struck a rich vein of silver in two of our mines. The richest in either Marus or Palatia. If Alexx invests now, he'll make a solid profit."

"Tezst will kill you for doing such a thing."

"He need never know it was me. I won't sign the note."

"It's trouble."

"Maybe, but I doubt it. When is the master supposed to return?"

"In three days, I heard."

"Good. He'll still have time to secure his investment."

The three days came and went in a blur of work. When Alexx and his wife, whose name was Sedras, were expected to return from their trip, Tezst ordered the entire staff of slaves and paid servants—about 30 in all—to line the front foyer.

They looked like a military parade as they stretched from the wide, marble staircase to the double front doors.

"Eyes to the front!" Tezst shouted as the front doors were opened. It was raining outside, a heavy downpour. A coach pulled up to the porch steps. A heavyset man in a gray military uniform, like those worn by the men in the field, stepped down from the coach. He quickly ascended the steps and, framed in the doorway, nodded stiffly to Tezst and then entered.

James and Glennall exchanged glances. Alexx was the man in the dream they'd both had in the mine shaft.

A woman appeared from behind Alexx. She also was heavyset, and she had a pinched, disapproving face and hair pulled back in a tight bun. She wore a large, hooded cloak fastened at her neck with a jewel. Underneath was a wide dress of satin that hid the movements of her legs. The effect made her look as if she floated on a cushion of air.

"Welcome home, Mistress, Master," Tezst said.

"Thank you, Tezst," Alexx said. "It is good to be back."

Tezst guided Alexx and Sedras toward James and Glennall. "We welcome you with two gifts from your good friend Valad," he said by way of introduction. "Two slaves from Marus."

"Indeed? From Marus?" Alexx said. "Oh, how kind of Valad."

"I wonder what he wants from you," Sedras said cynically. As they continued across the foyer, she stepped on a slick of water, and suddenly her legs flew out from under her skirt and she fell flat on her bottom.

Everyone gasped. James thought she looked like someone straight out of a Charlie Chaplin film. The sight made him want to laugh.

"My dear!" Alexx cried out as he and Tezst helped her to her feet.

Embarrassed, she shouted, "What kind of servants do we have when the floors are covered with water?"

"We must've brought the water in with us," Alexx observed calmly.

"Greater care should've been taken!" she shouted, nearly slipping again. Alexx and Tezst grabbed her elbows quickly. James had to put his hand over his mouth to keep from laughing out loud. This caught Sedras's attention. "Are you *laughing?*" she demanded.

James stiffened his mouth. "No, ma'am," he said, instantly serious.

"*Madam*, you ignorant creature," she hissed. "I am a *madam*."

James corrected himself. "*Madam* – er, no, Madam."

"I think I should like to see you soundly whipped!" she shouted again. She jerked her arms away from her husband and Tezst. "Let go of me! I'm not an invalid." She took another step and slid again, this time forward into James and Glennall. They both caught her.

In that moment, James was no longer standing in the foyer but deep in the core of the earth—in a mine. He was stripped to the waist, digging into a solid wall of stone. Black dust fell around him, filling the air, filling his lungs. He coughed. Next to him, Glennall also dug. Sweat poured from both of them. They had been working for hours. Days. Weeks.

Glennall turned to him and said, "Evil intentions, good consequences. The Unseen One will see to that. But it will get worse before it gets better."

"What?" James asked.

"I said to unhand me!" Sedras snarled. Her face had gone pale, as if she'd seen a ghost.

James was confused. He looked at Glennall.

Glennall looked startled.

They had shared another dream, another vision.

"I want to go to my bedroom immediately," Sedras said to her husband, a lamentable tone in her voice. "I'm not feeling well."

"Yes, dear," Alexx said. "It's been a long journey."

Tezst signaled two chambermaids to accompany Sedras to her room.

After she'd been whisked away, Tezst glared at James and Glennall, but he spoke to Alexx. "My most profound apologies, Master," he said. "I'll have these two beaten immediately."

"For what?" Alexx asked.

"For daring to lay hands on the mistress."

"She had fallen, Tezst. They were trying to help."

Tezst gestured to James. "This one seemed to find her predicament amusing."

Alexx gave James a sympathetic look. "*I* would have been amused, too," he declared, then added wearily, "but if I'd laughed, she would have punished me in far worse ways than you can ever punish them. Forget the incident. Let's get on with our work." With that, he walked off toward his study.

Tezst clapped his hands to dismiss the servants. James and Glennall started to leave, but he grabbed their shoulders. "The master was in a good mood today," he fumed. "But you had better watch yourselves in the future. Another incident like that and I'll personally thrash you."

James was getting ready for bed when Glennall crept into his room. They hadn't had a chance all day to talk about what had happened.

"Well?" Glennall said, sitting on the edge of the bed.

James was tired and wanted to go to sleep. "Well, what?" he responded crossly.

"Are you going to deny it?"

"Deny what?"

"The vision. You saw it, I'm sure. The two of us, slaving in the mines."

"I saw it."

"What do you think it means?"

James answered glibly, "It probably means we're going to wind up slaving in the mines."

Glennall nodded. "The Unseen One is warning us."

"Warning us about what?" James asked impatiently. "In one dream, Alexx is commending us for something, and in another dream we're slaving in the mines. I wish your Unseen One would make up His mind."

"One dream doesn't make the other untrue."

"Then what does it mean?"

"It means exactly what we think it means: We will be praised and then punished."

"Praised for what, and punished for what?" James climbed under his covers, using his feet to push Glennall off the bed. "It's a lot of hooey."

Glennall didn't reply.

James suddenly had an idea. "I know what'll happen," said. "We'll get punished because *you* were messing around with the master's desk."

CHAPTER EIGHT

The next morning, just as James and Glennall finished chopping the wood, Cowen appeared at the back door. He had an anxious look on his face and wrung his hands nervously. "Come quickly," he instructed. "Tezst wants the entire staff to meet in the kitchen."

"Is something wrong?" Glennall asked.

"Come quickly. Don't dillydally." Cowen retreated back into the house.

"Uh oh," James said as he stuck his ax into a log. They went inside.

The entire staff had assembled around the large kitchen. Tezst made a grand entrance, marching back and forth in front of them with a dark look of disapproval on his face. "Who did it?" he finally asked.

Everyone looked at the others fearfully.

"Did what, sir?" one of the older servants asked.

Tezst held up a piece of paper. "Who wrote *this* to the master?"

James felt the blood rush from his face. It was the note Glennall had written.

The tension in the room felt alive, like a buzzing bee on a windowpane.

"Someone had better answer soon or I will systematically beat the truth from each of you."

Glennall stepped forward and confessed, "I am the author of that note, sir."

Tezst looked unsurprised. He grunted. "I could have

guessed," he said as he walked over to face Glennall. "Come with me."

"Where are we going?" Glennall asked.

Tezst clipped him on the side of the head. "You dare to ask me questions? You are going to see the master. And then I will take great relish in beating the living daylights out of you." Tezst marched him to the kitchen door, then turned to face the uneasy crowd again. "Go back to your duties."

"Oh my," Cowen muttered.

James returned to work. A little later, as he was sweeping one of the upstairs hallways, he saw Tezst come out of Sedras's room. He looked surprised to see James there.

"Are you spying on me?" he demanded.

"No, sir. I'm sweeping the floor," James replied meekly.

Tezst looked dubious, then said, "I have no doubt that you were in on your friend's prank."

James didn't reply.

"If I had my way, you'd both be sent to the mines. I didn't trust you the first time I set eyes on you."

James merely watched him. He figured that if he spoke he would get slapped again. Just then a bell rang.

"Ah, it's the master," Tezst said with glee. "He probably wants me to dispose of your friend."

Finishing his chores upstairs, James returned to the kitchen to help Ruislip with lunch preparations. He was peeling potatoes when Tezst came in and tersely announced that the master wanted the entire staff to gather in the front foyer. He left again before James could tell whether he was pleased or angry.

Assembled for the second time that day, the staff stood watchful and silent. A door slammed down the hall, and within seconds Alexx approached in his usual military gait. Glennall and Tezst followed behind in a small procession. *Soldiers on parade*, James thought.

"I have an announcement to make," Alexx said as he clasped his hands behind his back. "Young Glennall here will no longer be serving with you."

James felt the muscles in his neck tense. He balled his hands into fists.

"Instead," Alexx continued, "he will replace Tezst as the keeper of my accounts."

There was a collective intake of air from everyone present. Tezst maintained an expression of calm, as if the news made no difference to him.

"Of course, Tezst will continue to manage the household and serve in his many other functions. You will answer to him as always," Alexx added. He paused as if he had something else to say, then turned on his heel and marched back to his study.

Tezst clapped his hands. "Back to work!" he ordered.

The crowd dispersed. James rushed to Glennall. "Congratulations!" James said happily.

"Yes," Tezst said. "Congratulations. I didn't enjoy being a *bookkeeper* anyway." He said *bookkeeper* as if it were the same as shoveling manure. He walked off.

Glennall waited until Tezst was out of earshot, then said, "Alexx thought my advice was too good to be true. So I explained to him who I am and how I knew."

"What did he say?"

"He said he had somehow suspected that I was from good breeding," Glennall replied with a hint of self-importance. "Then we chatted about a few financial strategies, and the next thing I knew, he put me in charge of his accounts."

"But if he knows where you're from, why won't he return you to your family?"

Glennall shook his head. "Palatians don't think that way. I'm a slave, regardless of my background. However, if I do well as his accountant, I may be able to earn my freedom."

"It's perfect."

"Unless I don't do the job very well. Then he'll probably kill me."

"Oh." James looked at him warily. "*Can* you do the job?"

"I can certainly do it better than Tezst did." He dropped his voice to a low whisper. "I think Tezst was juggling the books, stealing money from the master."

"He looks the type. It's those shifty eyes," James joked. He glanced around. "I'd better get back to work before he realizes I'm still talking to you. He's probably itching to give me a beating since he can't beat you now."

Glennall smiled. "He can't beat *you* anymore either," he said with obvious satisfaction.

"Why not?"

"Because I persuaded Alexx to make you my assistant."

"You're kidding."

"You'll still have various jobs to do around the house—fetch me new ledgers, make sure my inkwell is filled, things like that. But you answer to me now. Not Tezst."

James laughed. "That's super! Thanks!"

Glennall moved toward the kitchen. "Let's go."

"Where are we going?"

"Our first job is to go to town to buy new jackets."

"Why new jackets?"

"Because we're not just house servants anymore. We're special, so we don't have to wear the regular gray jackets. Alexx wants us to have silver jackets instead, just like the one Tezst wears."

"And just like we saw in our dream," James added.

"Which dream is that?" Glennall asked, feigning igno-
rance. "Or do you mean the dream you don't believe in?"

James blushed.

In the weeks that followed Glennall's appointment as the
accounts keeper, James found himself busier than he'd ever
been in his life. He had thought being Glennall's assistant
would be easy. Instead, it meant that he had to run into town
regularly to deliver or receive messages about Alexx's investments. Glennall had also put James in charge of the house provisions, inventorying stocks of food and supplies to make sure
the master's money wasn't being wasted.

The master was ecstatic about Glennall's abilities and
James's hard work. The investments from Marus quickly yield-
ed more money than Alexx could have imagined.

One afternoon, he called the two of them to the front foyer
and in front of the entire house commended them. It was the
fulfillment of the first dream James and Glennall had shared.

Tezst kept a stony expression on his face.

Sedras, the master's wife, cooed and fawned over the two of
them and made a public declaration of forgiveness. "I haven't forgotten how you two naughty boys behaved the first time I met
you," she said. "But all is well now. You've made my husband
very happy and prosperous. And if he's happy, then I'm happy."

Alexx kissed his wife's hand. "You are a treasure," he said.

Later that night, Alexx was summoned to the king's palace
to discuss matters of state. Glennall decided to use the master's
study to go over the ledgers and asked James to join him. It
was their habit for James to sit near Glennall at the desk and,
like a secretary, write down a list of things Glennall thought

should be done with various accounts and investments. It was a warm evening, so they opened a window and enjoyed the sound of the crickets outside.

"This is a pretty good life, isn't it?" James asked.

Glennall was only half-listening. "Pretty good for a couple of slaves, I suppose," he answered.

James leaned back in his chair. For him, it was pretty good by any standard.

Someone knocked gently on the door, and then it opened. To their surprise, Sedras entered the room. She wore an elegant, green velvet dress with a lace collar and large cuffs on the sleeves. Her hair was drawn off her face into a bun, and ringlets dangled in front of her ears.

Out of respect, Glennall and James leaped to their feet.

"Hello, boys," she said with a thin smile as she drifted around the room. "Hard at work, I see."

"Yes, madam," Glennall acknowledged.

She seemed to float up to the desk. "You're so very hard-working and efficient," she flattered.

"We do our best," Glennall said.

"Yes, you do." She chuckled lightly for no apparent reason, then said, "Sometimes, though, I wish you weren't as good as you are."

"Madam?" Glennall asked, puzzled.

"Your efficient control of my husband's money is making it very hard for me to get at it."

"You have money," Glennall reminded her. "Your husband gives you a generous allowance."

She rolled her eyes as if burdened by his response. "But it simply isn't enough," she insisted.

"Then you should talk to your husband."

"He's such a bore about these things," she said, stifling a

yawn. "It would please me so much more if you would give me extra funds."

"I can't without his permission."

"You could if I made it worth your while." She smiled at them. "And I *could* make it worth your while."

Glennall clasped his hands behind his back, as Alexx so often did, and stiffened his back. "We're not interested," he said softly.

"Aren't you?" she said, false surprise in her voice. "Are you saying you *don't* want your freedom?"

James felt his mouth go dry. He tightened his fists at his sides, the knuckles going white like the feather on a quill pen.

Glennall spoke, but there was a catch in his throat. "You're offering us our freedom?"

"Of course. Serve me well and I will serve you well. It's the way of the world."

"Only the master can free us," Glennall observed.

Sedras waved her arm as if she could brush the words from the air. "I need only speak to the master and he'll do it."

"If it's so easy to persuade him," Glennall said doubtfully, "why don't you speak to the master about your need for more money?"

She chuckled again as she leaned on the desk, a polite smile frozen on her face. Her tone was thick with anger. "Don't toy with me, boy," she threatened. "I know more about you than you think. I know who you are and where you come from. I also know that the two of you engage in some sort of witch-work."

"Witch-work!" James exclaimed.

"The day you both touched me, I saw a vision. A vision of both of you in the mines. It was as real to me as you are now."

"What about it?" Glennall asked coolly.

"You both have some kind of magic in you. I believe you could use that magic for me."

Glennall shook his head. "It doesn't work that way."

"Confound it, boy, do you want your freedom or don't you?"

"Not if it means deceiving the master. We wouldn't dream of betraying him. Nor would I betray my allegiance to the Unseen One by doing what you ask. It's wrong."

"You Marutians are so self-righteous," she said with a scowl. "And look where it's put you, *slave*."

Glennall didn't respond.

She sighed and walked to the door. "I can be a good friend," she said, "but I am a worse enemy. I have the power to make the vision of the mines come true." With that, she left.

"That's bad news," James said. He tugged at his collar. The room suddenly seemed hot.

Glennall swallowed hard. His hands shook nervously. "May the Unseen One protect us," he whispered.

"You did the right thing," James assured him. "I don't trust her any farther than I could throw her."

Glennall looked puzzled over the statement, as if he wanted to ask James *why* he would throw someone. Instead he said, "Will you hand me the ledgers from the past year? I want to look again at Tezst's bookkeeping. Something tells me that if he was embezzling money from the master, he might have been doing it for *her*."

James went to the shelf where the ledgers were kept and began to pull out a couple of them. His mind was buzzing with a question. When he put the ledgers in front of Glennall, he asked, "Why does a woman like that need more money than she already has? It's not like she's hurting for anything."

"Perhaps it's sheer greed," Glennall speculated. "Or she's up to something."

"She's up to something, all right. But what?"

CHAPTER NINE

Glennall sent James into Muirk the next afternoon to deliver instructions to Alexx's bank manager. The manager told James to come back in an hour for a return message. James decided to use the time to get a better look at the city.

Walking along High Avenue, as they called it, he enjoyed the sights and smells of the bakeries, the butcher shops, the fresh vegetable stands, and the fish shops. He also saw clothing stores, weavers, tailors, and tobacconists, all nestled in among offices containing lawyers, doctors, and businessmen.

His eye caught a colorful sign at the end of an alley, and James decided to follow it. "Win or Lose," it read. A bright arrow pointed the way. He wondered what kind of shop could allow someone to win or lose—or *what* one could win or lose there. As he approached the door, it opened, and Tezst stepped out. His brow was furrowed, and his mouth turned down as he glared at James.

"What are you doing here?" he demanded.

James stepped back for fear the man might strike out at him. "I'm running errands for Glennall," he replied.

"Well, you'd be well advised to forget you saw me," Tezst said. "Now get out of my way," he added as he pushed past James. His boot heels clicked loudly as he strode down the stone pavement toward the avenue.

James looked at the door of the Win or Lose shop. He had no doubt what it was. "A gambling joint," he said to himself.

Glennall was consulting with the master for the rest of the

afternoon, so James didn't have a chance to tell him what had happened with Tezst. He moved around the house impatiently, certain the accidental meeting was important. What if Tezst had been stealing from the master to pay for his gambling losses? But then, what did that have to do with Sedras?

"Why do you pace like a lion in a cage?" Cowen asked him when he'd wandered into the kitchen for the fifth time in an hour.

"I need to talk to Glennall."

"About what?"

James eyed Cowen for a moment, trying to decide whether to tell him. He decided not to. "Something private."

"Private I understand," Cowen said, his head nodding precariously in front of his stooped body. "We all have things we keep private."

James's face betrayed the question mark in his mind. "What are you talking about?" he asked.

"I'm saying only that there are things to discuss out loud and other things to be said in whispers." The man closed his eyes, his head still bobbing up and down. "I've been watching you ever since you arrived."

"And avoiding me, too," James added. "You haven't said two words to me since that night you gave me the ointment for my muscles."

"Things must be done in their proper time."

"What things?"

"Talking, planning, hoping, praying ..."

James was beginning to think the man had gone senile.

Cowen poked a bony finger into his chest. "I know about you. The hand of the Unseen One is upon you."

"Oh, really?"

"It's in the color of your eyes. It's in the blessings you've received. Do you think they're accidents? No. But the time is coming for you to go home."

"I *am* home," James responded, meaning every word. He felt settled now. Secure. It was the most at-home he'd felt since his parents died. "This is my home now," he repeated firmly.

The old man *tsked* disapprovingly. "This is not your home."

James decided to see just how much the man knew. "If this isn't my home, then where is it?"

"Not here. Not even in Marus. You come from other parts."

"Would you mind if we quit playing this game and put our cards on the table?"

The old man looked quizzical, then said, "You don't belong here. And the time is coming for you to leave."

"*Leave?* You think I'm going to try to escape?"

"Ah," Cowen answered with a smile, as if enjoying the thought. "Escape. Perhaps we all will. Perhaps the Unseen One sent you to us for that purpose, to help us escape what is to come."

James had lost his patience. "You keep talking in circles," he scoffed. He turned and pushed through the door into the main part of the house. As he did, he nearly collided with Tezst.

"Watch where you're going, boy," Tezst snapped.

James apologized and continued on his way to the study. By the time he reached the door, he had begun to wonder if Tezst had heard any of the conversation. He thought no more about it, though, because the study door was open. Glennall sat at the desk, the quill feather jerking as he wrote.

"Done with your important meeting?" James asked.

Glennall didn't look up. "The master and his wife had a dinner engagement in the city this evening," he responded. "We'll continue tomorrow."

"I need to talk to you."

"You'd better close the door."

James did, then sat down in the guest chair facing the desk.

Glennall stood up, stretched hard, then sat down again. "I figured out how Tezst stole the money from the master," Glennall said. "He lied about the amounts of food and supplies he was buying for the house."

"Did you tell the master?"

"Not yet. I plan to tell him tomorrow—*if* I can come up with a sensible explanation for why Tezst, a man well cared for and in one of the best positions in the country, would steal like that."

"I think I have the answer."

Glennall raised an eyebrow.

"Gambling," James said.

"What makes you think so?"

"I saw Tezst in the city today. He was coming out of a betting shop. I was thinking: What if he has a problem with gambling? You know, what if he can't control himself? And then he loses his money and has to raise even more."

Glennall shook his head in disbelief. "Tezst? He doesn't seem like the kind of person who'd do that."

"I'm just telling you what I saw today. Why else would he be there unless he was gambling his money away?"

Glennall rested his elbows on the desk. "Which gambling shop did he go to?"

"The Win or Lose, in an alley off High Avenue."

"I need you to go back there. Tell whoever is in charge that you're on an errand for the master. Warn him that if he doesn't cooperate, the security forces will descend on his shop like a terrible plague."

"The owner won't believe me."

Glennall snatched up a piece of paper and quickly scribbled

a note. He then sealed it with Alexx's stamp and handed it to James. "Give him this," he instructed.

"What will you do?"

"Finish putting together my evidence from these ledgers. Then I'll show everything to the master tomorrow morning." Glennall smiled. "Well done, James."

It took James 20 minutes to run to the edge of the city and another 10 to weave his way through the shortcuts that got him to the center. By the time he had reached the door of the Win or Lose, it was locked. He knocked anyway. No one responded. He continued to knock until his knuckles hurt. Then he saw a rope for a bell to the right side and began pulling it again and again. If anyone were inside, the noise would be annoying enough to force him to open up.

Sure enough, James soon heard the door unlatch from the other side. It opened a tiny crack, and a young man peered out at him. "What do you want?" the man inquired. "We're closed."

"I'm here on behalf of the head of the security forces," James replied.

"You're lying," the young man said with a frown and started to close the door.

James wedged his foot in. "I'm not lying," he insisted. "And you'd better open this door or you'll have no end of trouble with the security forces." He thrust Glennall's note at the young man.

The young man looked at the seal, opened and read the note, scrutinized James for a moment, then said, "What's Alexx want with me? To place a bet? Ha! Everybody knows he hates gambling. So what does he want with me?"

"I'm here to ask about his servant."

"Tezst. What about him?"

"He was here earlier today."

"So?"

"How often does he come in?"

"That depends on whether the missus has any money."

"The missus?"

"Alexx's wife."

James tried to keep his composure. "Tezst is here to bet for *Sedras?*"

The young man frowned again. "You must be a stranger. Everybody knows the missus likes to bet. Well, everybody except Alexx. She's done a pretty good job of keeping it from him."

"Until now."

"You're going to tell him? Good luck."

James headed back up the alley.

The young man shouted after him, "Tell Alexx his wife owes us a lot of money. Personal checks accepted!"

The entire way back to the mansion, James tried to decide what to do. It was one thing for Tezst to steal from the master to support a gambling problem of his own. It was another for the master's *wife* to have the problem. How would he react to the news? Would he be pleased that Glennall and James had uncovered the truth? Or would he angrily hold it against them for bringing to light an embarrassing and potentially scandalous piece of news? James hoped Glennall hadn't done anything yet. They needed to talk it over first.

James knew something was wrong as soon as he arrived at the back door of the mansion. Valad, the officer who had purchased James and Glennall as a gift for Alexx, was in the kitchen with some of his men. Two of them had Glennall by the arms. Tezst stood in the corner with his arms folded and an indignant look on his face.

Even more surprising was that Alexx and Sedras, dressed in their fancy dinner clothes, were standing near the door.

"What's going on?" James asked.

Rough hands were quickly on his arms and shoulders as Valad's men grabbed him.

Glennall looked helplessly at James. His eyes moved to a small stack of money on the table.

"We'll ask the questions here!" Valad growled.

"You're making a big mistake," Glennall told them.

"I'll be the judge of that," Alexx said. He looked stern and unhappy.

"I knew they were nothing but trouble," Sedras complained. "It was their lack of respect."

Glennall pleaded, "Master, please hear me out."

Alexx pointed to the money on the table. "What was my money doing under your mattress?"

"I don't know," Glennall replied. "Someone must've put it there."

"*You* put it there," Sedras said. "After you stole it from my husband."

"I didn't!" Glennall cried out. "Why would I?"

Tezst stepped forward hesitantly. "I regret to say that I might have the answer to that question," he offered. All eyes turned to him. He looked grieved to speak the words. "I overheard *this* one"—he gestured to James—"talking to one of the other servants about escaping. Since these two boys are like peas in a pod, it's easy to conclude that they stole the money to buy their way back to Marus."

"That's not true!" James shouted. "We aren't trying to escape!"

"You deny talking to Cowen earlier about escaping?" Tezst challenged him. "Or do you call me a liar?"

James didn't answer for fear that it might get Cowen in

trouble. His mind raced for something to say, but he couldn't think of anything.

Tezst shrugged and turned to Alexx. "There you are. His silence is the same as an admission."

"This is a setup," James finally muttered.

"We didn't steal any money," Glennall sneered at Tezst. *"You're* the one who's been stealing from the master. You have been for months!"

"Where is your proof?" Alexx asked.

"In your ledgers! I can show you how he did it."

Alexx looked unconvinced. "But why? Why should Tezst steal from me? He's a free man. He may come and go as he pleases. He is more than adequately compensated for his work here. And a more frugal man I've never met in my life."

"And you're welcome to search my apartment," Tezst said confidently. "Produce evidence of money I've stolen or anything I've ever purchased with such money."

"Has he told you about his gambling problem?" Glennall said to Alexx.

James cringed as the room went coldly silent.

Tezst looked aghast. "He's obviously willing to say *anything* to get out of this trouble," he suggested. "I promise you, master, that I have no such problem."

Alexx leaned toward Glennall. "You'll have to come up with something better than that to persuade me!" he warned. "Tezst is no gambling man."

"*He* may not be a gambler," James put in nervously, his heart pumping like a rabbit's, "but someone else is!"

"What are you saying?" Alexx demanded.

"Tezst goes to the gambling shop to place bets for someone else."

Glennall stared wide-eyed at James.

Sedras took a step forward. Her face was pale, her eyes flashing defiantly. "*Who* is he acting for, boy?" she barked.

James tried to swallow, but his throat was dry. The effort made a harsh clicking sound. "You!" he croaked.

Sedras stumbled back dramatically as if James had struck her. "*What?*" she shrieked.

"You go too far, boy," Valad said.

Sedras waved her hands like fans. "I must sit down. This is too much for me." She clung to a chair. James thought it was an impressive performance.

Alexx moved around the table. His face was red, though a slight scar across his forehead shone white. "You're accusing *my wife* of gambling?" he asked. "And not only gambling, but using my trusted servant to do so? And ... and ... of *stealing* from me to support her activities?"

James knew then that their situation was hopeless. It was too much to expect Alexx to believe. All the proof in the world wouldn't convince him.

"We would never lie to you, sir," Glennall said softly.

Alexx turned on him. "And my *wife* would lie to me? My trusted servant, who has been with me for years, would lie to me?" His brought his fist down hard on the table. "I've heard enough. Dress them in their old clothes. I don't want to lose those new uniforms. Then take them away, Valad."

Valad signaled his men, and they yanked the two boys to their feet.

"But where are we going?" James asked. "Where are you taking us?"

Valad looked to Alexx to answer the question. Alexx turned his face away from them all. "To the mines," he replied.

CHAPTER TEN

The journey to Palatia with Nosz now seemed like a family picnic compared to Glennall and James's trip to the mines. After Valad had dragged them from Alexx's mansion, they were taken to a decaying building in the city center where they were handed over to a wiry, greasy-haired man named Cleo. The moment Valad was out of sight, Cleo took great pleasure in thrashing both boys with a stick. He said nothing but cackled happily. He then kicked at them until they cowered in the middle of the floor. At that point, he threw a switch and a trapdoor fell open, sending James and Glennall to a dark room below.

They landed hard on a wet, stone floor. Winded, cut, and bruised, they lay silently for a moment. Then they realized they were surrounded by other prisoners. Men, women, and one or two children, all in rags, stared vacantly at them.

One of the men laughed and said in a low, gruff voice, "New recruits." A toothless old man laughed with him.

"Any broken bones?" James gasped to Glennall.

With great effort, Glennall sat up and replied, "I don't think so."

"Quiet down there!" the wiry man shouted from above.

They spent the entire night and the following day in that dank hole. Occasionally the trapdoor opened again, allowing more prisoners to fall painfully into their midst.

James felt cold and ill. He hoped he wasn't coming down with a terrible disease, but he wouldn't have doubted it considering the stench and germs that now surrounded him.

The next afternoon, the large, wooden door at the end of

the pit opened. Three muscular men entered with muskets. A fourth man stepped in with a whip in his hands. With a great display of whip cracking and gesturing with the muskets, they chained the prisoners' ankles and wrists, then drove them from the room to a tunnel. The look and smell made James think they were in a sewer somewhere. At the end of the tunnel, they reached an oversized and windowless wagon. Six mangy horses were hitched to the front. Once or twice, James felt the sting of the lash on his back as they were herded into the wagon.

There was hardly room for them all. Sitting down was impossible, so the prisoners stood there, pressed together, smelling of sweat and rotten clothes and other disgusting things.

Once they were all squeezed in, a driver shouted "Yah!" followed by the sharp crack of a whip. The horses lurched forward.

"Where are the mines in Palatia?" James whispered to Glennall.

"In the southern mountains," Glennal whispered back.

"How far are the southern mountains from here?"

Glennall seemed unsure. Then: "Four days in a wagon."

"They won't keep us cooped up in here the whole time, will they?"

Glennall looked away.

"They'll give us water and some food, right?"

"I hope so," Glennall said hopelessly.

The prisoners eventually worked out a system whereby they could take turns sitting down. A woman wept constantly, her wailing high and shrill.

The road jostled them into each other. James did something he never thought he could do: He slept standing up. But that was a luxury; sleep rarely came. Mostly he thought about how thirsty he felt and how tight his stomach was getting.

"May the Unseen One have mercy," Glennall whispered

hoarsely at one point.

James closed his eyes and joined in the prayer. *Have mercy*, he said in his heart to the Unseen One. When he was living in the comfort of Alexx's mansion, it had seemed easy to scoff at Glennall's belief. But now, in chains, thirsty and tired, such faith seemed like the only thing that could help them.

Late in the afternoon on the third day, they heard a distant crash of thunder. Soon after, they heard rain tapping on the wagon's roof. Then the water began to leak through. The prisoners clamored to stretch up their hands and faces to drink in what they could.

As night fell, the rain stopped. The air got cooler as the wagon made its way into the mountains. James dreamed he was back at Aunt Edna's, eating some of her apple pie.

Someone shook his shoulder. Aunt Edna and her apple pie disappeared. "James, wake up. James!" It was Glennall.

James opened his eyes. Bright sunshine poured into the wagon. And he was not standing up but was stretched out on the floor. "What happened?" he asked, sitting up quickly. The wagon was half empty. The other prisoners were filing out the door.

"We're at the mining camp."

James got out of the wagon and felt his heart sink. The camp was a collection of rundown shacks sitting on a clearing of dirt.

"Line forms to the right," a guard bellowed repeatedly. The prisoners' chains were removed at this point, but since they were stiff and sore, James and Glennall still hobbled to the line, which paraded past a long table. There they were given a flea-infested blanket, a crudely made bowl, and directions to the shack that would become their new home. "You *might* find a straw mattress to sleep on, if you get there fast," they were told by a man behind the table.

James and Glennall made their way along the dirt paths, past the armed guards, to their rickety shack. It was a ramshackle construction of rotting wood, with gaps in the planks large enough to allow a small child to crawl through.

"This'll be cozy in the winter," James said as he stepped inside.

A dozen men were already there. Three sat at a wooden table in the middle, playing cards. A rusty stove sat in the corner, around which several men lay on their mattresses. One mattress was left for James and Glennall to share.

A guard suddenly appeared at the door. "What are you doing?" he shouted at the men playing cards. Quick as a flash, his whip was out, flicking at the men, who scattered. "We don't like cards in this camp!" he declared. "They make men lazy."

Some of the men grumbled their apologies as they cowered behind the table.

The guard coiled his whip again. "When the bell rings, you can get your grub at the canteen," he announced.

"Food?" James asked, his stomach hurting now from four days without it.

The guard snorted, "As close to it as you'll get in this pit."

When the bell rang, James and Glennall rushed down to one of three stone buildings in the camp. Inside they joined a line for plates of food, then sat at one of the long tables. The food consisted of some kind of boiled meat, rotting potatoes, and a biscuit infested with weevils.

James bit his tongue to keep from crying.

◆———————◆

That night as they tried to go to sleep, Glennall said, "Don't be discouraged, James. We'll get out of this."

"Yeah? What makes you think so?" James asked moodily.

"The Unseen One will get me out of here. And where I go, you'll go."

James looked at him skeptically. "Why should the Unseen One get you out of here?"

"To make things right with my brothers."

"You mean so you can get back at them."

Glennall pressed his lips together but didn't speak.

"Why do you think the Unseen One cares about that?" James continued. "Why should He care about us at all?"

"He does. You were not brought here for this. I think you've been sent here to be my helper."

"To help you get revenge? Not me," James said, shaking his head. Then he frowned. "Besides, what makes you think everything circles around you and your stupid revenge?"

"What do you mean?"

"You think the Unseen One is going to do what you want, and He's sent me to help you do it. What makes you so arrogant? The world doesn't spin around you."

"James," Glennall said confidently, "for as long as I can remember, I've known that the Unseen One has chosen me for something remarkable. I have a purpose, a destiny to fulfill. Meeting you has made me more sure of it than ever."

"That's *your* opinion," James replied. But suddenly he doubted himself. How could he know whether Glennall was right or wrong? "Anyway … you don't have to get cocky about it."

"I know two kids who're going to get their ears boxed if they don't go to sleep!" said a harsh voice nearby.

As James fell asleep, he heard someone in the camp play a pipe. The tune was low and mournful.

At sunrise the next morning, a guard arrived and screamed at them to get out of bed, cracking his whip randomly around the cabin. They were all led to the canteen again, where some brown, gravylike slop was thrown on plates in front of them. Afterward, they were taken to another stone building. A group of men called inspectors poked and prodded them to check their physical condition.

"You're in the mines," one of them said to Glennall.

Another slapped James hard on the arm, as if he were slapping the rump of a horse. "You'll do for a runner," he concluded.

"I don't know what a runner is, sir," James replied.

"You'll find out soon enough."

The room suddenly went quiet as a man entered. He was middle-aged, with a waxen face. He wore a broad-brimmed hat with a large feather sticking out of the side. His coat and breeches were black, offset by a white shirt with lace collar and cuffs. His boots were also black, but they were polished so that the dim light reflected off them. He held a walking stick.

"Who is that?" James whispered.

The inspector who'd slapped his arm replied, "It's Estburn, the keeper of the camp. He's boss over us all. Mind your manners with him if you don't want to be hurt."

Estburn strolled through the crowd of prisoners, inspecting them as he went. "So you are our newest members," he said without warmth. "Welcome."

He paused in front of a tall, lanky man with a thin face, beaklike nose, and stringy, gray hair. James recognized him as one of the men who'd been playing cards the day before. "You are Bask," Estburn said.

The man bowed slightly but spoke with a posh accent and an air of superiority: "I am, Your Eminence."

"Fell out of the king's favor, did you? Served him a bad piece of meat?"

"It was all a misunderstanding, which I hope to have resolved very soon."

"We shall see about that," Estburn replied. "Meanwhile, you will use your cooking abilities in *our* humble kitchens."

"Yes, sir."

Estburn turned his gaze to the man next to Bask. He was an average-sized man, another card player from the day before. His expression was taut and proud. He stood straight and sturdy like an iron bar. Estburn smiled at him. "Chalcer."

The man bowed stiffly.

"The king must have been in a bad mood that week, to send us his prized chef *and* the head of the palace police."

"I have been unjustly accused by my enemies," Chalcer said.

"Isn't it always the case?" Estburn said in a mocking tone.

"Where may I best serve the master of this camp?" Chalcer asked politely.

"A man of your strength and determination will serve us best in the deepest part of the mine."

Chalcer frowned.

"Unless you have a complaint about our choice for you?"

Chalcer bowed again. "I am here to do your bidding."

Estburn leaned close to him. "And you will, my friend, I assure you." He continued through the crowd of prisoners, stopping in front of James and Glennall. He eyed Glennall from head to foot, then turned to James. His expression registered the same surprise James had seen on the faces of others who'd looked at him. "Well, well. You're a treat," he said.

"Sir?"

"Eyes of two different shades. How unusual."

Estburn walked on. He didn't stop to speak to anyone else, but James thought he saw him exchange a quick glance with another prisoner: a short, thin man with narrow eyes and deep wrinkles around his eyes and mouth. There was something knowing about the look they exchanged, but James had no idea what it meant. He recognized the man as the third card player from the day before.

Mining tools—a pickax and a bucket—were distributed to most of the prisoners, Glennall included. Since James was a runner, he was given only a leather cap with a small lamp in it.

"But what does a runner do?" James asked another inspector.

The man looked at him as if he'd asked a stupid question. "He *runs*, you twit," he stated.

Guards directed them out of the stone building and up the dirt path to the main entrance to the mine.

They were soon at the mouth of the entrance tunnel. A large shack stood off to one side, and on the other side were three hoists with cages attached to heavy ropes. James saw groups of miners get into the cages, which were then lowered into the main vertical shaft by three men at three different wheels. They turned the wheel one direction to lower the cages, then reversed it to bring them back up. Sometimes they let the miners in, and other times they brought the coal out in buckets and wheelbarrows. The ropes were marked to indicate the lengths needed to reach the different levels of the mine.

"Miner?" a guard asked Glennall.

He held up his pickax and bucket and nodded.

"Get in," the guard said.

Glennall squeezed into the cage with other miners. Slowly it descended out of James's sight. He watched the rope as it went—taut and strained—and shivered. It looked unsafe.

The guard shouted at James, "What's your purpose in life?"

"I'm a runner," James answered.

The guard hooked a thumb in the direction of the shack beside the tunnel. James walked over to a stocky man with a shaved head and scars on his forehead.

"A runner, eh?" he said after James explained why he was there.

"Yes, sir, but I don't know what a runner does."

"Simple. You run things into the shafts for me. If a miner needs a new pickax, you run it down. If a miner needs a new candle for his cap, you run *it* down. And when you're not running down, you're running back up, bringing me reports on their work and samples of the ore they find. Got it?"

"Yes, sir."

The man then handed James a box of candle wicks and ordered, "First job today, take these to level four, shaft three. And be quick about it. I don't tolerate laziness."

"How many levels are there?" James asked.

"Seventeen."

"But that's like drilling into the center of the earth," James observed.

The man coughed. "I know."

The rest of the day, James exhausted himself running in and out of the various tunnels and mine shafts. A bell rang for the men to take a 15-minute break for lunch; then it rang again to send them back to work. The same bell rang several hours later to signal the prisoners to end their work. Another bell would ring shortly to beckon them to the canteen for supper. James waited by the cages for Glennall to come up. It felt like the end of the first day of school.

Glennall eventually stepped out of one of the cages, barely resembling the boy who had gone down in the morning. His face and clothes were covered with black coal dust and streaked with sweat. He walked slowly, stiffly, coughing sporadically. But he didn't complain. He didn't even speak until they were almost back at the cabin.

"Now I see what I never saw before," he said grimly.

"See what?" James asked.

"This is how we treat the workers and slaves in my father's mines." His eyes were red-rimmed. "Once the Unseen One has made things right with my brothers, I will change things at home. No one should spend another day like this, let alone a lifetime."

James wondered if Glennall's attitude was to be admired or pitied. *If we get out of here,* then *he should be admired,* James concluded. *But if we're trapped here for good, I feel sorry for him.*

As they approached the cabin, they heard shouts coming from inside. Stepping through the door, they took in the scene immediately: Chalcer stood in front of one of the men who shared their cabin—a scruffy old coot called Onei. Chalcer shook his fist in the man's face. "You stay away from me and you stay away from my things!" he threatened.

Onei spread his arms. "I don't know what you're talking about," he insisted.

"You're either a thief or a spy for Estburn. I don't care which it is, but you'd better stay clear of me!"

"You're out of your mind."

Chalcer grabbed Onei's shirt with both hands and pulled him close. "Stay clear!" he hissed in Onei's face. Then he thrust him away.

Onei staggered and kept his balance only by grabbing the wooden table. He looked around at the circle of faces gazing on him in silence. Embarrassed, he pushed through the wall of men and stomped out the door.

"Was that wise?" Bask asked Chalcer calmly.

Chalcer dropped onto a chair and began to take off his boots. "I won't put up with it," he said indignantly.

"But if he's working for Estburn, you may wind up in trouble."

"Estburn had better kill me then. If I suffer because of that little rat, he'll suffer, too. I'm as good as dead if the king leaves me in this camp anyway. I have nothing to lose." He wiped a dirty sleeve across his dirty brow. It smeared the coal dust with more coal dust.

"I agree with Bask," Glennall said to James later. They had gone to a large collection of troughs in the center of the camp where the prisoners could wash up. The water was filthy and cold. "Onei makes my skin crawl, but there's no point in making Estburn angry."

James splashed the water on his face and arms. He couldn't tell whether it made any difference.

Glennall continued as he wiped a rag over his body, "Estburn may be useful to us."

James stifled a laugh before responding, "I think you've been breathing too much coal dust. We're *slaves* in this camp, and you talk about Estburn like he's going to serve *us* somehow."

"He might."

"And pigs might fly."

"Stranger things have happened," Glennall said earnestly.

"Uh oh," James said.

Two guards had come to the canteen door. Their eyes searched the room, filled with prisoners eating their gruel, until their gaze fell on Chalcer.

"I knew it," Bask said despondently as they approached down the aisle between the long tables.

Chalcer looked up from his plate at the two gorillalike men who positioned themselves on both sides of him. "Don't

I get to finish this delicious dinner?" he asked glibly.

The two guards grabbed his arms and dragged him from the canteen.

"What will they do to him?" James asked.

Bask shrugged and replied, "Beat him, whip him—I'm new here myself, so I don't know. But I knew it would happen this way. Didn't I tell him?"

Across the room, Onei finished his meal without ever looking up.

The two moons were framed by the open window on the side of the cabin. James lay next to Glennall on their shared mattress. Glennall's breathing had settled into the steady rhythm of someone in a deep sleep. In other parts of the cabin, people snored. Everyone was exhausted.

James was exhausted, too, but he couldn't sleep. His mind retraced the events that had taken him from being an orphan at Aunt Edna's to being a prisoner in a mine. He wished now that he was back there with the old woman. *She isn't really as bad as I've made her out to be,* he thought. *All she wanted me to do was behave myself, study my lessons, and go to church with her. Was that so awful? Probably not. But at the time, it seemed like the worst life in the world. Now, lying on a damp, flea-infested mattress in a slave camp, things sure look different.*

Aunt Edna was a deeply religious woman. James suspected that she prayed morning, noon, and night, if not all the time. Now he wondered what she would think about all the dreams and visions and the legends of the Unseen One. Would she believe them? Probably, which might be one reason he was so resistant to them. His mother and father had rejected everything to do with the church. They were "rationalists," they said. Life and the world could be explained within the realms of science and nature. God was no longer needed, and faith was a waste of time.

James felt a ball of emotion rise in his throat as he thought about his parents. He missed them terribly. But he also began to think they had been wrong. There was nothing scientific or natural about what had happened to him. He had suddenly shifted from one world to another, the color of his eyes had changed, and now he seemed to have this strange, special ability to have visions about things that would happen.

Glennall had said it was because of the Unseen One. He'd said James was there to fulfill some kind of purpose. But *what* purpose? To help Glennall? If that were true, why didn't the Unseen One just come out and tell him what he was supposed to do?

Aunt Edna always said that "God works in mysterious ways." So if the Unseen One was like the God of his world— or was in fact the same God—then maybe He also worked in mysterious ways. Through dreams and visions?

Glennall was convinced the Unseen One would get him out of the camp so he could get even with his brothers for what they'd done. It put a fire of hope in his eyes, a determination on his face, that few of the other prisoners had. But James wavered. Glennall might be right, or he might be completely wrong. Did the Unseen One help some people so they could get revenge on other people? Did God?

Aunt Edna had once said that God was love and justice all wrapped up in one. James had dismissed the idea. "It doesn't make sense," he'd told her. "Love is one thing, and justice is another. How can love and justice be wrapped up together like that?"

"That's the mystery of *grace*," she had replied. And then she had smiled at him in that pinched way she had.

James sat up.

"Dreaming?" Bask asked, sitting at the wooden table in the shack, pulling on his boots. Morning light filled the room.

James shook his head. He had fallen asleep after all.

At that moment, Onei ambled up to him. "You should get your breakfast while it's hot," he suggested. Then he leaned uncomfortably close and added quietly, "Estburn wants to see you and your friend in his office after the work bell rings tonight."

Just then, James saw Chalcer walk in. His gait was stooped, and he moved his legs as if he had a great weight on them. The side of his face was swollen and purple. He stopped where he was and looked in their direction. But he wasn't interested in James. He was gazing with hatred at Onei.

It began to rain while the prisoners walked up to the mine. When they arrived at the mouth of the tunnel, James was told by the man with the scars on his forehead that he wasn't needed for running. He was then given a pickax to help dig in the mines.

"Level two," the man said.

"That's my level," Glennall said happily.

An hour after they started digging, James was coughing uncontrollably. Black dust filled the air, blew in his face, and coated his lungs. Sweat dripped and stung his eyes. He glanced over at Glennall, who was also bathed in sweat but wore that expression James now knew so well: a look of clenched teeth and nerve. He would not complain. He would not show his pain or suffering.

Glennall turned to him and said, "Evil intentions, good consequences. The Unseen One will see to that."

And James remembered that that was exactly how it happened in the vision they'd seen when they both tried to stop Sedras from falling.

"Take my hands," James said abruptly as he put down his pickax.

Glennall looked around quickly to make sure a guard wasn't near. To stop working would usually result in a sharp whip across the back or a club on the head.

"Come on," James persisted.

"You know it doesn't always work."

"I know, but I want to try." His heart was pounding hard. "I want to believe the way you do, *hope* the way you hope."

"You should believe even if we don't see anything."

"Maybe I will," James responded, but he kept his hands held out. "Take my hands anyway."

They grabbed hands.

Instantly the mine disappeared and James and Glennall stood in a great crowd of people. Their arms reached out to Glennall, their faces yearning. At first James thought they were thronging around him in adoration, applauding him for some reason. But then he realized they were begging, beseeching him to help. Their faces were thin, their cheekbones prominent, their eyes sunken. They were starving. Hundreds of them, maybe thousands.

Then, just as suddenly, the crowd was gone and the boys were back in the mine again.

The two looked helplessly at each other.

"It will get worse before it gets better," Glennall said simply.

Just then, a guard shouted at them from farther down the shaft, "Boy!"

James and Glennall both turned.

"Not you," he said to Glennall, "I'm talking to the runner."

"Yes, sir?" James responded.

"You're wanted topside to do some more running. Lucky you."

"Yes, sir," James replied and started away.

As he went, James heard the guard tell Glennall, "Which means *you'll* have to work twice as hard."

"Lucky me," Glennall said with a sigh.

Navigating his way through the mine, James reached the cage just as it was arriving from the upper level.

"I'm going down," Onei said, stepping into a spot of light. "Use the other cage."

"All right," James said as the cage started to move down.

The cage stopped for a second, then slipped three or four feet.

"Something's wrong," Onei said, his face a confused blend of that same smile and now worry.

James moved toward the cage. "Get out! Hurry!"

Onei took a step for the door to climb out. It was too late. The cage suddenly dropped, disappearing into the hole, free-falling downward.

Onei's scream echoed through every shaft and tunnel until it was cut off by the sickening crash of wrenched, splintered wood at the bottom.

James slumped against the cave wall, oblivious to the men who came rushing from the different shafts. He cupped a hand over his mouth to keep from vomiting.

Glennall was at his side. "Onei?" he asked.

James nodded, squeezing his eyes shut. He tried to block out that final expression on Onei's face before the cage fell. But it stayed with him for a long time after.

CHAPTER ELEVEN

❧———————❧

"The camp inspectors have told me the rope had worn out. It was frayed, and it broke," Estburn said to James and Glennall. They were in his office, having gone there directly when the bell rang for the workday to end. The rumor throughout the camp was that Chalcer had taken his revenge on Onei for the beating Estburn had given him.

Estburn lived and worked in the third stone building, the smallest of the three. It was a strange mixture of stone and wood that reminded James of a hunting lodge he had once seen in a magazine. Estburn stood before the two boys in an outfit of purple—purple jacket, purple breeches. His shirt had a lace collar and sleeves, also embroidered in purple. A purple hat with a white feather sat on his desk.

James and Glennall sat on two wooden chairs, their hands in their laps. Glennall had instructed James before coming in that they must always appear respectful and *never* look Estburn in the eye. A man like him might consider it a challenge to his power and have them whipped.

"Enough about the unfortunate accident," Estburn said. "I will miss old Onei. But, like everyone in this camp, he can be replaced. I'm interested in the two of you mostly."

"How may we serve you, sir?" Glennall asked.

"By answering my questions honestly," he replied. He walked around the desk and sat down in his chair. James stole a glance at him. Without his hat, his head looked small. His brown hair was thinning, and his pink scalp peeked through in patches. His eyes were greenish and narrow, set beneath a heavy brow. His nose was puglike, and his lips were two slivers of pink set between thick jowls. He would have been comical if he hadn't had so much power to be cruel. "Tell me about yourselves," he instructed once he was comfortably seated.

James waited for Glennall to speak, but he didn't.

After a few awkard moments, Estburn continued, "I'll make it easy for you. I know that the two of you are not Palatians and that you're here because you tried to steal from Alexx, the head of the king's security forces."

"We didn't steal anything, sir," James said defensively.

Estburn smiled. "I'd be quite happy if you stole from Alexx. There's no love lost between us."

James looked up in surprise.

Estburn chuckled. "That's right. You may both look up. I don't think much of cowering."

Glennall slowly raised his head.

"As I was saying," Estburn went on, "Alexx is no friend of mine. He was responsible for giving me this position as keeper of the prison camp."

James wondered why Estburn was telling them all this. He worried when adults told their youngers too much about themselves; it usually meant they wanted something.

Estburn added silkily, "I never cared for Alexx's wife, either. What was her name? Sedras, that's right. A woman not to be trusted."

James and Glennall didn't acknowledge or deny the comment.

"I understand you were both very helpful to Alexx for a time. What did you do for him?"

"We helped him with his accounts," Glennall replied.

"How?"

Glennall explained about how he had invested Alexx's money, managed his accounts, and kept his house in good financial order.

When Glennall had finished, Estburn said, "I'm impressed that someone your age was so resourceful. Can you help me in the same way you helped Alexx?"

Glennall was confused. "In what way, sir?"

"The king requires camps like this to be profitable for him. He wants the workers to be productive for his kingdom, generating a lot of coal and ore not only for Palatia, but also to export to other countries. I would like to impress His Majesty, if possible."

"We will be pleased to help in any way we can," said Glennall.

Estburn clapped his hands together. "Excellent! You may spend tonight drawing up a plan for me."

"Tonight?" James asked. He knew Glennall was exhausted from his day's work, and so was he.

"Tonight," Estburn affirmed. "If I like what you propose, you may not have to go to the mine tomorrow. If, however, you produce a lot of rubbish, I'll have you beaten *and* sent back to the mine. Do I make myself clear?"

"Yes, sir," the boys replied in unison.

"And if I catch you stealing from me, you won't live to regret it. Understood?"

"Yes, sir."

Estburn left them. The instant the door was closed, Glennall was on his feet and pacing quickly.

"What are we going to do?" James asked, worried.

"We're going to come up with a plan," Glennall replied. "Get a pen, ink, and paper ready, James. You'll be my scribe."

James obeyed. And for the next six hours, they discussed

and argued ways to make Estburn's mine a profitable enterprise. For the most part, Glennall modeled the plan on how his family had revived a failing mine on their property. Step one was to find new sources of ore. Step two was to find more efficient ways to get the ore out of the earth.

"Those cages have to be replaced," Glennall said.

James thought of the silent Western movies he'd seen and did his best to explain how the coal was brought out of the mines in them. He scribbled drawings of railway tracks and carts. Glennall thought James was a genius and decided they could build tracks on every level, leading to a shaft with one of the cages that would be used only for hauling coal to the surface.

Step three was to figure out how to change the prisoners from slaves to workers.

"He'll never accept that," James interjected.

"We'll try anyway," Glennall said. "Everyone will work harder if they know they have a *reward* waiting for them at the end instead of a whip—or death."

"What kind of reward? Everybody around here wants freedom."

"Maybe freedom for some, maybe better accommodations for others. Maybe we should devise a system of payment, a way for the workers to put wages away for the day they're released." Glennall's eyes were bright with enthusiasm. "There are dozens of things we can do!"

They filled several pages with ideas.

By the time they finished their plan, the clock on the wall showed two o'clock in the morning. Numb from exhaustion, they stepped out of the office door to falling rain and a sleeping camp. A guard waved a musket in their direction. "I'd better escort you or you'll get shot," he said.

They trudged through the darkness and the mud to their shack. Then they stepped inside and watched the guard walk away. The room seemed unusually still. James noticed that no one was snoring. Was it empty?

Suddenly he was grabbed. Hands seemed to come from all directions, pulling him one way and another, then down onto the floor. Someone lit a lamp, and James saw he was surrounded by the men who shared the cabin. Glennall was also pinned to the ground.

"What's the big idea?" James cried out.

"Be quiet!" a voice said.

"Where have you been?" another voice asked. It was Bask.

"Shut up, all of you," a third voice chimed in. This one belonged to Chalcer. "Light another lamp, but keep it dim."

Flint was struck and another lamp lit.

"Bring them to the table," Chalcer commanded.

The two boys were carried to the table and dropped into two of the chairs.

"What's the meaning of this?" Glennall asked.

"That's what *we* want to know," Chalcer said. "You go off to see Estburn, and what do we think? You're being beaten for something. Instead, though, you return to us at two in the morning without a scratch on you. What have you been doing, reporting to him about us? Are you his new spies now that Onei is dead?"

"It's none of your business," Glennall spat.

Chalcer slapped him and commanded, "Try again!"

Glennall stubbornly tightened his lips. He wasn't going to answer. Chalcer raised his hand again.

James quickly said, "We weren't spying!"

"Then what were you doing?" Bask chimed in. "Wining and dining with him?"

"No, we were—"

"Don't speak!" Glennall interrupted firmly. "It's none of their business. If they want to hurt us, they'll have to answer to Estburn."

Chalcer was unimpressed. "You two want to go the way of Onei?" he threatened. "Is that what you want?"

"Kill us and you'll be killing any hope for this camp," Glennall said coolly.

"What does that mean?" Bask asked.

"You'll have to wait and see."

Chalcer growled, "I'll get it out of you!" He grabbed James's left hand and Glennall's right. He was going to twist their wrists, expecting that the pain would make them talk. But instead, he froze where he was, his face suddenly going hard as if he'd had a great shock.

James and Glennall knew why, for in that moment, they saw what Chalcer saw in his mind.

Chalcer stood in fine robes of state made of thick, purple velvet. A man whom James had seen only in paintings at the house of Alexx and around the shops of Muirk stood before Chalcer; he wore a royal robe of white. It was King Akvych. A gold circlet sat on his close-cut, white hair. His face was clean-shaved and had the stern expression of a man who knew power well. He held his hands over Chalcer—as if in a blessing of some sort—and announced to the gathering that Chalcer had been exonerated after being falsely accused and was now restored to his rank as the chief of palace security. The crowd around them applauded. Then the clapping and the picture itself faded away. They were all once again in the flickering shadow of lamplight.

Chalcer stared at the two boys with an expression of fear. He let go of their wrists. "What kind of magic was that?" he demanded.

Glennall didn't answer. He only smiled confidently.

"What happened?" Bask asked. The rest of the men whispered anxiously to one another.

Chalcer kept his eyes on the two boys. "I've heard whispers about you two," he said in amazement. "You see things in dreams."

"It's true," Glennall replied.

It might have been James's imagination, but he thought everyone except Chalcer suddenly took a step back from them.

"Then explain to me what we just saw," Chalcer instructed.

"I think it's obvious what we saw," Glennall offered. "You will be returned to the king and restored to your former position."

Chalcer's face seemed to soften from relief. "When?"

James remembered something. In the scene, Chalcer had had a healing scratch on his forehead, up near his hairline. The scratch was visible on Chalcer's forehead now. "You'll go back to the king before that scratch heals," James said.

Glennall looked at James, clearly impressed.

Abruptly, Chalcer turned to the men in the shack. "Put out that light," he ordered. "Go to bed."

"But what about these two?" Bask demanded. "What about their connivings with Estburn?"

"Forget about it." Chalcer went back to his bed.

Bask and the rest lingered for a minute as if waiting for someone else to take charge. No one did. Then the lamp was put out and everyone returned to bed.

James noticed two things the next morning. First, Chalcer seemed nicer to James and Glennall than he'd ever been before. He said "Good morning" to them and even offered to let them use some of his toothpaste, an expensive commodity in that place. Second, Bask seemed to linger near him and Glennall as they prepared for the day. Bask was normally up early to help cook the breakfast at the canteen, but this morning he moved slower, with a forced casual air. Only after everyone else had left and James and Glennall were about to leave the shack themselves did he approach them.

"I want to know what's going to happen to me," he said abruptly.

"We're not fortune-tellers," Glennall explained.

"But I saw what happened to Chalcer last night," he persisted. "He's not easily impressed by anything. But the look on his face ..."

"It's not within our control."

Bask licked his upper lip. James noticed there were beads of sweat on it. "I've been having terrible dreams lately," Bask said nervously. "I want to know what will happen to me."

James raised an eyebrow to Glennall, who shrugged.

Bask's mouth twitched into a smile. He held out his hands to the two boys. "Come on."

"This is not our doing," Glennall said as he took Bask's left hand. "It's up to the Unseen One to reveal or not reveal."

James took Bask's right hand and immediately wished that he hadn't.

The room was filled with the stench of decay. They weren't in the shack anymore, however, but in a dungeon somewhere. The walls were slick and mossy, dripping foul water. Somewhere overhead was a dim light. It was like looking up a tunnel. Iron bars crossed a rectangular hole in the ceiling.

They heard a rhythmic creaking sound. James turned in its direction and saw Glennall standing next to him. Glennall looked ill, as if he'd seen something that had made him sick. The creaking continued, steady, swaying. It reminded James of the time his father had tied an old tire to a tree branch for the children to swing on. When they did, it creaked in the same way. It was the knot of rope rubbing against itself and the wood.

James looked beyond Glennall in the direction of the creaking sound. There he saw a man's body tied by the neck to a scaffold. The body swung slowly. The dead eyes bulged, and the tongue hung out. It was Bask.

"No!" Bask cried as he pulled his hands away from the boys. He looked at them angrily, a fury in his voice when he finally spoke again. "You are charlatans! You're playing tricks with my mind! The king would not execute *me*." He spat at them. "You're worse than fortune-tellers. Stay away from me, you frauds!"

He left them in a rage.

"It's not our fault," James said to Glennall as they walked to the canteen.

Glennall sighed. "No, it isn't," he agreed. "But few people see it that way."

A guard intercepted them before they reached the canteen door. "The boss wants to see you," he informed them.

James felt queasy as they approached Estburn's office. What if their night's work didn't meet with his approval? What if he hated their ideas and beat them severely, as he had promised?

The guard opened the door to the office. "Go in," he ordered.

James was surprised to see both Chalcer and Bask waiting in the office as well.

"Well, well," Chalcer said.

Estburn entered by a side door, one that led from his private apartments in another part of the building, James guessed. Without looking at them, Estburn went to his desk. He didn't sit but stood looking down at various papers spread out before him. "I have news," he finally said.

The four of them waited.

He held up a piece of paper. It looked formal, with ornate writing and a splotch of red wax on the upper right-hand corner. James would learn later that the wax was the king's seal. "Miracle of miracles," Estburn said, looking up at Chalcer. "You are to be released to go back to the palace."

Chalcer clicked his heels together and gave a slight bow in acknowledgment.

Estburn then picked up a second piece of paper that looked like the first. "Bask, you're being called back to the palace, too," he continued.

"I knew it! The king has given me a reprieve!" Bask said happily, clapping his hands together. He sneered quickly at James and Glennall. "So much for your dreams."

Estburn smiled. "Actually, the king seems to have decided that you were in on a plot to poison him. He has signed confessions from three of your staff, two of whom are now dead by hanging. His Majesty has decided to execute you as well."

Bask's face went ashen. His mouth fell open in stunned surprise. "No!"

"Normally we would have obliged the king by executing you here, but His Majesty insists that you be hung in the royal dungeon." Estburn spoke as if he was describing a minor inconvenience.

Bask began to weep. "No, please, it's a mistake!" he cried.

At some signal James didn't detect, two guards entered and grabbed Bask's arms.

He resisted, but without effect. They dragged him from the room. "No!" he cried. "Please! It's a terrible mistake! I would never try to poison the king! I wouldn't!" He shouted similar things until his voice echoed in the open air outside, then faded, then suddenly stopped. James never saw him again.

"The king bids you to go immediately," Estburn said to Chalcer.

Chalcer nodded and moved toward the door.

"No hard feelings, I hope," Estburn said in a friendly way just before Chalcer left.

Chalcer didn't reply but turned to gaze at him with a deliberate and studied expression. After a few seconds, he faced James and Glennall. "I will not forget the two of you when I am back in the palace," he said. And then he was gone.

Estburn cleared his throat.

It's our turn, James thought. *One bit of good news, one bit of bad news. Which will it be for us?*

"I'm intrigued by the plans you've drawn up," Estburn said, abruptly sitting down and rifling through the papers they had left for him.

James shifted uneasily from foot to foot.

Estburn glanced up. "Oh, don't be nervous. I want you to sit down so we can discuss what you've written. Some of these ideas are rather foreign, even radical. But they appeal to me. Sit down so we can talk."

James and Glennall pulled up the two visitors' chairs. Once again a signal was given that James didn't see, and a guard entered through the apartment door. He carried a tray bearing three plates of breakfast—not the gruel from the canteen but a real breakfast of eggs, bacon, ham, potatoes, and toast.

"I want you well fed," Estburn said simply when he saw the smiles on the boys' faces. "I want your minds *sharp* for the work you have to do."

Chapter Twelve

❦━━━━━❦

Somewhere outside the perimeter of the camp, spring turned to summer and touched the trees with green, the flowers with white, purple, yellow, and red, and the air with warmth and bird song. Inside the camp, it grew noticeably warmer. But the ground remained barren and muddy from the workers' boots. Inside the mines, the dark was still dark, the damp was still damp, and the coal dust still covered and choked the men.

Thanks to Glennall and James, other things changed. Their plan to make the penal colony a profitable enterprise took shape. Estburn got all the credit for their ideas, of course, but he was smart enough to reward the boys as well. He took them out of the shack and put them in a corner apartment of his stone house. It wasn't luxurious by any means, but it was better than they'd had: two honest-to-goodness beds, a washstand, a small potbellied stove, two writing desks, and a cupboard for the various papers and files they needed to do their work.

As had happened at Alexx's house, Glennall became the staff accountant. He pored over columns of numbers, watching over the stocks and supplies, expenses and income. He haggled with outside investors and carefully negotiated contracts to sell the camp's coal not only to the Palatians, but also to Marutians.

"I'm in competition with my own family," he said with a laugh from his desk one day.

"What do you mean?" James asked.

"We're both trying to secure business with the Albanites."

He was amused by the thought for days, but James knew he wasn't really happy. He had that look in his eye—the look of revenge.

James's role was to represent the workers. He met with them regularly to discuss their problems and difficulties, their needs and wants, and then report back to Glennall and Estburn. This gave him particular pleasure for two reasons. First, his father had once been a representative for factory workers near their home in Pittsburgh, back when the unions had power, before the Depression started. Second, the slaves began to feel less like slaves and more like regular workers. James argued hard to get more-sensible working hours, the shacks repaired, new mattresses brought in, healthier food in the canteen, proper plumbing and sanitation, and safer conditions in the mine. He used every idea he'd ever heard his father mention at the dinner table when recounting to his mother what had happened at the factory that day.

As long as Glennall could make it work financially, Estburn didn't seem to care. He was content to sit and enjoy the profits.

Summer came so gently that James hardly noticed the increase in temperature, the mugginess of the days, or how the men had stripped down to their undershirts to do their work.

One day late in June, a young man knocked on the door of the boys' apartment, then came in. It was Barric, a servant of Estburn's whom James and Glennall had befriended. Not only was he good company, but he often brought them the latest rumors from Estburn's office as well. Of more importance, James and Glennall found him invaluable for helping them to navigate around Estburn's various moods.

On this June day, Barric stood before them with his hands clasped in front of his gray apron—he'd obviously just come from Estburn's kitchen—and a smile stretched across his handsome face. His brown eyes sparkled.

Glennall was sitting at the desk, doing sums on a page of inventory, and hardly noticed Barric at all. James eyed their friend from his own desk, where he was working on a crude drawing of the mine, trying to devise a better means of getting the coal out.

"What are you smiling at?" James asked.

"Estburn has been invited to the palace," Barric answered.

Glennall looked up. "He has? Why?"

"The king is having a banquet to reward successful businessmen in the country. Estburn is going to receive a special award for what he's done with this camp."

"What *he's* done!" James harrumphed.

"None of our ideas would have been carried out if Estburn hadn't approved," Glennall reminded him.

James harrumphed again.

Barric continued to smirk. "Your friend Chalcer is also going to receive an award."

"Oh?"

"Apparently he exposed some spies in the palace who were selling Palatian trade secrets to other countries." Barric paused for the sake of drama, then added, "I heard that your old master was part of it."

"Alexx—a spy?" Glennall said. "I don't believe it."

"It was his wife, actually," Barric explained. "She was selling secrets to help pay for a gambling problem she has."

James and Glennall stole a glance at each other.

Barric continued, "Anyway, Alexx has had to resign in disgrace. His wife will probably be jailed—or executed."

"That's too bad," James said sincerely.

Glennall leaned back in his chair. "I wonder how Chalcer

and Estburn will get along? You can be sure Chalcer hasn't forgotten that beating."

"Maybe not, but he seems to have forgotten *us*," James observed.

"He made no promises to us," said Glennall. "Besides, it isn't as if we did him any favors. All we did was let him see what was about to happen to him."

The banquet at the palace was two weeks away. Estburn pestered Glennall and James the entire time. He wanted to make sure he had all the facts and figures in his head so he could impress the court with his knowledge of the camp's success. He rehearsed his speech in front of them and, fortunately, took their advice to cut it from its original length of 20 minutes down to a polite "thank you" and a brief statement of how grateful he was to the king for the honor.

Finally the day came. Estburn and Barric in their best outfits, two guards, and a driver piled onto the horse-drawn coach and hurried off.

Glennall and James watched them leave, then turned to go back into their apartment. Somewhere in the camp, they could hear fiddles and other kinds of stringed instruments playing. Men were shouting and dancing. The smells of various barbecues filled the air. In a large, level place, some of the men played their version of what James knew as soccer. These were the sounds and smells of a Sunday, the only day when all the slaves were free to enjoy themselves. That was one of the changes James had made: no more working seven days a week. Though this world didn't seem to understand the idea of a Sabbath or of going to church, James had it fixed in his mind from *his* world that one day should be free of work, and that day should be Sunday.

Some of the men shouted for James and Glennall to join in

the sport. "We're short by two!" they called. "Come on!"

"I have work to do," Glennall said.

"Forget your work. Take a day off," James encouraged as he rushed off to join the game.

Glennall glanced toward the apartment, then laughed. "All right," he agreed.

During the afternoon, as they kicked at the ball, raced around the field, and nearly killed themselves trying to score a goal, James was aware of how much they'd both changed. Glennall was no longer the pasty-faced noodle he'd been when they first met in the cave. He was becoming a strong, intelligent, and handsome young man. James didn't consider himself handsome, but he certainly felt older and more responsible than the boy he'd been at Aunt Edna's. He even appreciated the fact that Aunt Edna's nagging at him about hard work and discipline might not have been such a bad thing after all.

At one point, James playfully tackled Glennall. They wrestled in the dirt for a moment, much to the amusement of the other workers. When Glennall got the better of him, James laughed and cried, "Foul!"

Glennall stood, extending his hand to James to pull him to his feet.

When their hands clasped, everything around them changed. The men disappeared. The camp was deserted. The shacks, so newly repaired, looked worse than they ever had: Roofs were collapsed, walls were fallen down, and doors were off their hinges. Wild dogs, thin and diseased, sniffed around for food. A rat scurried away toward the stone buildings, which were mere shells now. The camp had been left to ruin.

"What happened here?" James asked Glennall, who stood nearby.

"They weren't prepared."

"Prepared for what?"

Then a deep voice shouted, "Are you two playing or not?" and James and Glennall were standing back on the field. The men watched them curiously. By now they had all heard about the boys and their "powers," but none had witnessed it firsthand.

"I think I've had enough," Glennall said. He waved to the men and walked off toward the stone building.

James did the same. When they were out of earshot of anyone else, he asked, "What did it mean?"

"I don't know," Glennall replied.

"What did you mean when you said they weren't prepared? Prepared for what?"

"I don't know."

"But—"

Glennall turned on him, annoyed. "James, I *don't know* what it meant."

"You don't have to get mad."

Glennall paused at the door of their apartment. He took a deep breath as if to control himself. "I'm sorry. I'm not mad at you."

"Then what's wrong?"

"I'm scared."

James understood. Some of these visions had left him feeling terrible and apprehensive. "I know why *I'm* scared, but why are *you* scared?"

"Because I think something horrible is going to happen."

"To us?"

"To the whole world."

CHAPTER THIRTEEN

———◆———◆———

The light in his eyes woke him up. James winced, then squinted. "What? What's wrong?" he asked.

"Get up. Hurry." It was Barric. He stood next to James's bed, still dressed in his best clothes and a long overcoat.

On the other side of the room, two guards whom James had never seen before were trying to get Glennall up.

"What's going on?" Glennall asked sleepily. "Barric, what time is it?"

"Two in the morning," Barric said. "Get your things together." His tone was low and serious. "I have to take you away *now*."

"Take us where?" James asked as he sluggishly swung his legs off the bed. "Where's Estburn?"

"He's still in Muirk. But he'll be coming soon."

"He sent you for us?"

"No. Chalcer did."

"Chalcer!"

"Yes. Look, there's no time to explain. I'll tell you everything in the coach."

"We can't just *leave*. Not without papers," Glennall protested. "This is a *prison* camp. We could be executed for trying to escape."

"I have your papers. Chalcer arranged everything. Now hurry up!"

James had no difficulty in packing. He'd always known that if he left the camp, there'd be little he'd want to take with him.

"Bring your ledger books and all your papers about the camp's finances," Barric instructed Glennall. Glennall obeyed. He would have taken the ledger books anyway. For him, they were the only proof of his abilities.

It had started to rain by the time they were dressed, packed, and loaded into the coach. James noted that it wasn't Estburn's coach but a royal coach from the palace, with the king's seal of two lions around a crest of blue and gold on the door. James felt as if he might be swallowed up by the seats, the cushions were so thick and soft. The driver urged the horses on to the prison gate. Barric said a few friendly words to the guard there, who was equally puzzled by the middle-of-the-night activity. He snapped to attention, however, when he read the papers. After a moment of fiddling with stamps and signatures in the guardhouse, he flagged them on.

For the first time in months, James and Glennall were beyond the camp fence. The mountain air was crisp. The moons were stark, penetrating the shadows and sharply defining the trees against the pale night sky. And unlike Glennall and James's arrival at the camp in a decrepit prison wagon, they were leaving it in luxury—a luxury they didn't understand.

Glennall leaned toward Barric. "What's this all about?" he inquired.

Barric's face was hidden in the darkness of the coach. "I'm a friend of Chalcer's who was sent to the camp to keep an eye on things," he explained.

"A friend," James said blankly.

"A *spy*," Glennall noted.

Barric didn't deny it. "It was no coincidence that I arrived to serve Estburn after Chalcer returned to the palace. Chalcer wanted to know what Estburn was up to."

"Why should Chalcer care about a prison camp official?" James asked.

Glennall smiled darkly. "No doubt Chalcer was looking for a way to get back at Estburn for that beating."

"That may have been part of his intention. I don't know. My instructions were to watch out for you two."

"Us?" James and Glennall responded together, surprised.

Barric shrugged. "Chalcer was deeply affected by whatever had happened between you. And he imagined that Estburn would make use of you somehow. I was sent to see how and to make sure he didn't harm you."

"Is that why we're running away now? Was Estburn going to hurt us?" Glennall asked.

"Yes."

"Why? We haven't done anything wrong," argued James.

"No, but Chalcer has."

"What?"

"At the awards banquet tonight." Barric smiled. "I wish you'd seen it."

"Uh oh. What happened?"

"Well, Estburn got up to make his acceptance speech for the award. It was a rambling thing that went on for ages. Mostly he took all the credit for his accomplishments with the camp."

James rolled his eyes. "So much for a quick thank-you."

Barric continued, "Chalcer received his own award next— and then made public what a fraud Estburn is."

"He said so then and there?" James found it hard to believe.

Barric nodded. "He announced that all of Estburn's success was due to two young men he had back at the camp."

James's mouth fell open. "He told them about *us?*"

"Estburn was outraged, of course. He stood up and demanded an apology. The king seemed amused by the whole scene but insisted that Chalcer couldn't make such accusations without proof. Chalcer said he would offer proof."

"We're the proof," Glennall said.

"Yes."

"But why rush away in the middle of the night?" asked James. "Why not go in the morning?"

"Chalcer was afraid that Estburn would get to you first and either hide you away or worse."

"Kill us?"

"Yes. Estburn is a very prideful man, you know." Barric gazed out the window into the night. James suddenly realized he wasn't the same pleasant servant they'd come to know over the past few months. He was a purposeful young man. He continued without looking back at them. "As it turns out, Chalcer was right. Estburn called me to his room directly after the banquet and demanded that I rush back to the camp. He instructed me to lock you up in the mine until his return tomorrow. But since I work for Chalcer, I came back to free you instead."

"But we're not free, are we?" Glennall said.

"Not exactly. Chalcer wants you at the palace for the time being."

James nudged Glennall. "At least we're moving up in the world."

Glennall didn't respond. They rode on in silence for a few minutes.

James thought about it and then chuckled softly. "Estburn is going to be very surprised," he stated.

Barric smiled again. "Yes, he will be. After tomorrow, he'll probably be working in the mine himself."

"The other workers won't let him do that for long," Glennall observed.

"Exactly."

"We're here," Barric said, nudging James, who had fallen asleep.

James sat up in time to see them finish their drive along a wall that was at least 20 feet high. It stretched out behind them for three or four city blocks. They reached two ornate wrought-iron gates—or were they made of gold?—and were allowed to enter by two guards in uniforms of blue and gray. On the lintel above the gate was the king's crest, just like the one on the doors of the coach.

Turning through the gates from the main road, the coach headed down the main driveway to the palace. The driveway stretched a couple of hundred yards to the front of the palace, lit along the way by small lamps. They looked like small stars that had formed a procession to pay homage to the king. It was hard for James to see the surrounding grounds in the dark, but the front of the palace was ablaze with light coming mostly from the countless windows reaching to the left and right from the front doors.

Barric said, "Welcome to Muirkostle."

"Muirkostle?" Glennall asked.

"That's the formal name, the ancient name that goes back longer than anyone can remember."

"When we worked for Alexx, everyone simply called it 'the palace,'" Glennall recalled. "I didn't know it had a formal name." He stared out the window for a moment. "What kind of building is it?" Obviously, his interest in details was unaffected by the beauty of the place.

"It's several buildings," Barric replied as they slowly made their way down the driveway. "The original castle is there to the left. Even in the dark, you can see the outlines of the towers and turrets. They're made of solid Palatian stone, from the quarries of Beforshe, Offord, Middexe, and Suirk, which is why they're still standing after so many centuries."

Glennall grunted noncommittally. He wouldn't dare admit to the superiority of Palatian stones, as his sense of rivalry between Marus and Palatia was great.

Barric went on: "Breskin, King Akvych's great-grandfather, added the central section of the palace—the one you see directly ahead of us. It has over 100 rooms."

"The new wing, built by King Akvych's father, Williv, has 40 rooms. That's where the royal family lives, over there to the right."

"Why so many rooms?"

"The rooms in the main building are for state occasions, mostly. The Grand Reception Room, the Banquet Hall—which has a table long enough to seat 150 people—and the Throne Room all have different functions. I won't bore you with the details."

"How do you know so much?"

"I grew up here. My father was a captain of the palace guard."

Glennall jabbed an elbow at James, who was still gazing at the palace. "James, you're awfully quiet," he observed.

James couldn't speak. He couldn't take his eyes off the place. It was the biggest and grandest thing he'd ever seen.

They stopped in front of the doors, and Barric leaped out of the coach. "Wait here," he instructed.

"Don't you think it's amazing?" James asked Glennall.

Glennall sniffed with feigned disinterest. "It's gaudy and overdone—like everything in Palatia."

Barric returned and told them, "Come on."

They followed him through the front doorway, where two tall, black doors stood open on both sides, and into a high-ceilinged, circular reception area. There suits of armor and statues of past kings surrounded them.

"This way," Barric said as he gestured, and they walked to the right down a long hallway covered in gold-leaf designs, velvet wall adornments, paintings, and tapestries. The doors to all the rooms were closed except for one. At a glance, James saw a long room with crystal chandeliers, royal-blue carpet, light wood paneling, and chairs lined up facing one another. At the head of the chairs was a larger chair on a small platform adorned with red curtains. James guessed it was the Throne Room Barric had mentioned.

They suddenly turned down another hallway that went up a few stairs to yet another hall, then turned right and down a few stairs, then back up and along another lengthy passage. Finally they reached a door where Barric stopped and knocked gently.

"Come in," a voice said. James recognized it immediately as Chalcer's.

His room—an office—was average-sized, with plush carpet, dark wallpaper, and windows covered by closed curtains. Inside were a writing desk and several chairs. There was also a round table that James assumed was for meetings. Shelves lined the walls with rolled-up papers, loosely bound manuscripts, and leather-backed books. Chalcer sat at the writing desk. In spite of the lit lamps over his head, he still had a candle burning nearby. He put down his quill pen and stood up.

"Hello, young men," he said with a click of his heels and a sharp bow.

James and Glennall repeated the gesture as best they could.

"Your journey was trouble-free, I hope?"

"Yes, sir," Glennall replied.

"Good." He rubbed his hands together. "The king wants to see you first thing in the morning."

James and Glennall couldn't disguise their surprise.

"Why does he want to see us?" James stammered.

"There are things he wishes to discuss with you."

Glennall opened his mouth to ask another question, but Chalcer waved him down.

"No questions," he instructed. "I want the two of you to get some sleep first. In the morning, you'll be bathed and then given appropriate clothes to wear." He tilted his head toward Barric.

"Off we go," Barric said.

They walked down the labyrinth of halls for another five minutes. Two doors were open on opposite sides of the last hall they reached.

"Glennall, you're in the bedroom to the left, and James is in the one on the right." Barric waited in the center of the hall while the two boys went to their rooms. "Sleeping gowns are on the beds. Strip your clothes off and leave them in the basket next to the bathroom door. The servants will take them while you sleep. Fresh clothes will be given to you in the morning. I hope you sleep well."

James and Glennall smiled at each other, then retreated into their respective rooms. James closed the door behind him. Two lamps, one on the bedstand and another on a small table near the window, were the only light he had. He didn't undress but threw himself onto the large, inviting, four-poster bed. He sank into the downy mattress and gazed up at the canopy. The light flickered, giving only glimpses of a tapestry there. It looked like men on horseback fighting in a battle on a rich, green hillside.

They sure like their battle scenes, James thought.

It was the last thing he remembered thinking until he was awakened the next morning.

CHAPTER FOURTEEN

❖————————❖

Bathed and dressed in stylish but comfortable breeches, shirts, jackets, and new boots, James and Glennall were taken by Barric to the Throne Room James had seen the night before. In the daylight, it was even larger than he had thought. The walls were lined with gold tables, each with a glass-covered display of a vase or a clock or china of some sort. There was also a large, marble fireplace. The room was paneled, but inside each panel was a painting of someone in royal garb.

"Sit down in the two chairs nearest the throne," Barric instructed them. "Chalcer and the king will be in presently." He exited, closing the door behind him.

James could hardly control the butterflies in his stomach. "What does he want with us?" he whispered to Glennall.

"I think he'll want to talk about the camp," Glennall replied. "Maybe he's interested in how we made it a financial success."

"Do you think he'll give you a job?"

"Give *us* a job, you mean."

"No, I mean *you*," James insisted. "Look, you're the one who's doing everything. You don't need me."

Just then the door opened. Instinctively, the two boys stood up. It was the right move. Chalcer entered the room and stood to one side while another man came in. There was no doubt from his manner that he was the king. But James didn't think he *looked* like a king. Instead of the heavy royal robes James had seen in the vision, King Akvych now wore a pair of white breeches and matching jacket, black boots, a plain white

123

shirt, and a red vest. His hair was close-cut, and a thin, golden circlet sat lightly on his head. There was no mistaking the face, though. Milky white, smooth and clean-shaved, with a jaw set firm like stone.

King Akvych walked up to the throne on the platform and sat down. He wiggled his fingers at the two boys. "Sit down, please," he said. His voice was higher than James had expected it to be.

James and Glennall sat down again. Chalcer remained standing to the right of the king.

"I have heard wondrous things about the two of you," the king began. "The work you've done at the prison camp is most remarkable. But that is not why I've asked you to see me."

He paused to scrutinize the boys. James wriggled in his chair.

"There is another, more serious matter that we must discuss." He then put a finger to his lips as if he had suddenly remembered something. "But first, tell them the news, Chalcer."

Chalcer cleared his throat and announced, "The king, in his mercy, has pardoned you from any charges resulting in your imprisonment."

The king added, "In light of the things we have learned about our former comrade Alexx and his notorious wife, we cannot help but believe you are innocent of their accusations."

"Thank you, Your Majesty," James said happily.

"Yes, thank you," Glennall said.

James wondered if this also meant they were no longer slaves.

The king seemed to know what James was thinking. "You were brought to this country as slaves," he continued. "But you will not remain so. Stay with me for a time, not as slaves but as servants, and you will be rewarded with your freedom."

Again the two boys thanked him.

Glennall dared to ask, "How may we serve Your Majesty?"

The king eyed the door as if to make sure it was closed, then spoke more softly than before. "Chalcer tells me you have powers."

"They are not *our* powers, but only those abilities which the Unseen One has given to us," Glennall said calmly.

"Yes, I know all about the god of Marus—this *Unseen One*." The king's tone had an edge of impatience. "But you *do* have powers. Powers that gave Chalcer a glimpse into his future."

"We are not fortune-tellers, sire."

"I would not be speaking to you now if you were fortune-tellers. My court is overrun with so-called fortune-tellers and wizards and prophets serving gods of old and gods of new and the gods know what else. I'm sick of their advice."

"What is it that Your Majesty desires?"

The king sighed deeply. "Peace of mind."

"What troubles you, sire?" Glennall asked.

"I have daydreams that are nightmares. Or perhaps they are nightmares that are my daydreams." The king scrubbed his hands over his face wearily. "Either way, they haunt me day in and day out. No one can tell me why I'm having them or what they mean. Now Chalcer has suggested that I speak to you."

James swallowed hard. This was a test. What if the Unseen One wouldn't let them help the king? What would the king do to them if they failed?

Glennall spoke firmly. "King Akvych, we are not interpreters of dreams. We see only what the Unseen One shows us."

"Then let us hope that your Unseen One will show you what is in my mind." The king stood up—the boys leapt to their feet as well—and walked down to them. He grabbed one of the chairs and dragged it near to them. Then he sat down and held out his hands. "Here. Take my hands."

"Sire," James said, worried enough to speak, "we can't *make* it happen. It's not up to us."

The king looked at James. His eyes were moist. "If nothing happens, I am no worse off than I was before. If something happens, then maybe your Unseen One will help us to understand why I'm so troubled. Now take my hands."

The room seemed thick with silence. It hung around them like one of the velvet curtains. A clock ticked somewhere, probably under a glass case on a golden table. Chalcer stood where he was, watching them.

Glennall took the king's right hand in both of his. James felt a chill go up his back. He took the king's left hand in his. The king's hand was warm and smooth to James's touch.

Nothing happened. The clock ticked. The silence continued. The king looked at the two boys, then closed his eyes and sighed again. "I suppose it was too much to ask."

"I'm sorry, Your Majesty," Glennall said.

"Some other time, perhaps," the king whispered as he made to stand up. James and Glennall also began to rise.

They were all still holding hands, James noticed, as if the king needed their help to stand up. The weight of the king as he got to his feet caused James to lose some of his balance. He jerked a little toward Glennall. Glennall quickly slipped his right hand from the king's grasp and reached out to steady James. James stumbled enough for Glennall's hand to slip down his arm. Their hands touched.

Instantly, the three of them were no longer standing in the Throne Room but found themselves in the middle of a large field. To their left, they saw a herd of large, fat cows moving slowly toward a huge, blue lake. They were joined by enormous pigs, plump chickens, and other kinds of fowl. As this procession moved in their slow, herdlike way, they seemed to shrink, as if someone had let the air out of them. They got thinner and thinner. Their legs, now spindly, buckled underneath them. One by one, all the animals fell until there were none left to reach the lake.

Then James noticed that the lake itself was no longer blue but a stagnant pool of green slime and dead fish floating on the top.

"This is my dream," the king said to them, his eyes alight as if he felt joy to share it with someone. He pointed to the right. "Look there!"

James and Glennall turned to look. A field of grain stood before them, the tops blowing gently in the wind. Mixed in with the grain were trees bearing fruit of all kinds. Then the wind picked up in its intensity until it was a gale force beating the grain and the trees until they could no longer stand. The grain tore from the ground like weeds, the trees were uprooted as if an invisible hand had plucked them like brittle sticks, and they all blew away.

"You now see what I have seen," the king said. Then they heard a roar from the distance. "What is this?" the king asked, alarmed. "This is new. I have not dreamed it before."

A great crowd of people approached them, their arms outstretched, their faces thin death masks. They begged for food, for help. James remembered this scene—he had seen it before. But he realized now that these people weren't dressed just as Palatians, but also as Marutians and in clothes he had never seen before. It was as if the entire world had descended upon them.

"What can I do for you?" the king cried to the crowd as they clawed at him.

"We have lost everything! We have nothing left," the people shouted. "Feed us! Give us shelter!"

"I do not know what to do," the king said.

The people wept and wailed at them.

James had an idea. He said quickly to King Akvych and Glennall, "Something like this once happened in my world. A lot of people lost all their money, and many lost everything they ever had. It was called the Great Depression."

"Was there a war?" the king asked.

"No."

"A famine, then," Glennall said.

"No."

"Then how did they lose all they had?" the king asked.

"My father said they didn't save enough of it," James replied. For reasons that escaped him, he quickly added, "But my Aunt Edna said they didn't put it in the right places to begin with."

It seemed like a ridiculous thing to say, standing in the middle of the crowd like that. But the crowd and the field faded away, and James, Glennall, and the king were standing once again in the Throne Room.

King Akvych was visibly shaken, but he said decisively, "Now I understand."

Chalcer, looking worried, was at their sides. "Sire, what happened?" he asked. "Are you all right?"

Glennall fell back into his chair, in breach of the usual etiquette around a royal person. "Something terrible is coming," he said gravely.

"What's it going to be?" James asked, the words clicking dryly in his mouth. "How's it going to happen?"

Glennall shook his head. "A famine? Disease? Drought? It could be anything."

"What are we to do?" the king asked as he slumped into his chair.

Chalcer was bewildered. "Are you so sure it will happen? Maybe you've misunderstood what you saw."

"Did you misunderstand when *you* saw what would happen to you?" King Akvych asked as a sharp rebuke. "No, my friend. Before now I misunderstood what I saw in my dreams. But *now*—now I understand clearly. I must call my advisers. I must gather together the greatest minds in the country. We must think of how to prepare for this ... this catastrophe."

"With the greatest respect, sire," Glennall began, then shot a look at James, "I don't think your advisers will give you better advice than you received from James."

The king looked back and forth between the two boys expectantly. "I didn't grasp what he said. Explain it to me."

"Tell him your idea, James."

James felt nervous and put on the spot. "I'm not sure it was really an idea," he said. "It was just a thought."

"Tell him your thought, then."

"My world—er, the place I come from—had a terrible problem," James started hesitantly. "A lot of folks lost all their money, the banks had to close down, and people lost their jobs and were thrown out of their homes. Many starved."

"Just as we saw in the dream," the king observed.

"I guess so."

"What was your thought?" asked Glennall.

"I remember my father saying that it was because people didn't invest their money very well, they didn't put it in the right places where it would be safe. Then my Aunt Edna argued with him and said it was mostly because they weren't *wise* about their money to begin with. She said something like ..." He stammered again as he tried to remember what she said.

"Where people's treasures are, that's where their hearts are. So we must store treasures in a place that will last forever. Or something like that."

Glennall leaned toward the king, his eyes on fire. "Your Majesty, if we plan *now*—if we put stores of food and water away *now*—we may have enough to take care of the people when the trouble starts."

"Feed the entire country? It can't be done," the king scoffed.

"Not only the entire country, sire, but other countries as well," Glennall said. "Palatia is a rich and prosperous nation. If we stored away even a *quarter* of all we have, we would do well in a time of difficulty."

"It's an enormous task," Chalcer interjected.

Glennall shrugged. "It's better than starving to death."

"But *how* can we do it?" the king asked, his voice tense, his brow knitted.

"If I were Your Highness—which I am not, of course—I would divide the country into districts. Then I would put people in charge of those districts, like governors, to collect and assemble the stores from the people. They would report to Your Highness—or to someone Your Highness puts in charge of the plan." Glennall sat back. James thought he looked pretty pleased with himself.

The king looked thoughtful for a moment, then said, "I will consult with my advisers. Chalcer, call them together immediately." He reached out to touch the two boys approvingly but seemed to think better of it, as if he feared seeing another vision. "One is enough for the day," he said. And for the first time, he smiled.

CHAPTER FIFTEEN

L ater that day, James and Glennall were in one of the palace
gardens, playing a Palatian game that, for James, seemed
like a cross between baseball and croquet. Barric taught it to
them and then gathered some of the servants to play.

James had just scored a point when he saw Chalcer crossing
the large, green lawn toward them. James and Glennall dropped
their equipment and ran to him when he called their names.
"The king wants to meet with you again," Chalcer informed
them.

"Did he meet with his advisers?" Glennall asked.

"Yes. They all ageed that your plan is brilliant. It will be
put into effect immediately."

"Then why does the king want to see us?" James wondered
aloud.

Chalcer didn't answer at first. He clasped his hands behind
his back and began walking toward the palace, motioning for
them to follow. He looked grim. Finally he said, "Allow me to
explain something to you. The king had a son who was his
pride and joy. He died at 12 years of age." Chalcer glanced at
James. "Around *your* age, I think. But had he lived, he would
now be closer to your age, Glennall."

"How did he die?"

"A mysterious disease that none of the doctors could
cure." Chalcer was silent for another moment, then went on,
"The king was heartbroken by the death of his son. Now he
looks at the two of you and, I believe, he sees his son again."

"Why are you telling us this?" Glennall asked. "We have

no desire to try and fill the void left by his son."

"Maybe you don't. And I hope you would not try to exploit the king's affections."

"You'd stop us anyway," James observed.

"So I would."

"What does this have to do with our meeting with the king?" Glennall asked. Something was troubling him, but James didn't know what.

"You will have to learn that for yourself," Chalcer answered.

King Akvych was in his state chambers, which James quickly realized was a fancy name for his office. He was gazing out the window when Chalcer brought in James and Glennall.

"Ah, my two prophets," the king said amiably. "Come in and sit down."

"Only if Your Highness will sit," Glennall stated.

The king chuckled. "As you wish." He sat down behind his desk, a massive and ornate block of wood that James thought could have served as a wardrobe. The king folded his hands in front of him. "I have spoken with my advisers, and they thought highly of your plan. In fact, they thought it was pure genius. Of course, they don't all believe in dreams and visions or that this famine is coming, but they see the benefit of taking action just in case. Besides," he added with a smile, "I'm the king, and I said they have to do it."

Glennall tilted his head forward, as if bowing. "We are honored by your faith in the Unseen One and what he's revealed to us."

"You are to be honored still more."

"Sire?"

"I discussed with my advisers the question of *who* should

be my representative in carrying out these plans. I want someone who will meet with the governors of the districts, make sensible and prudent decisions, and oversee the entire business. I want someone who will be *me* to the people. Sadly, we could not think of anyone among our established ranks."

James's eyes widened as he suddenly realized what this meeting was about.

The king went on. "Then I realized that I must look outside our established ranks to make such a radical plan work the way it should. Which is why I decided that *you* should be my representative."

Glennall froze in place. Not a muscle, not an eyelash, not even a molecule moved.

The king laughed at his predictable reaction. "Don't you have anything to say?"

"I'm speechless, sire." Glennall shifted nervously in his seat. "I don't know what to say."

"You think you *can* do it, can't you?"

"I believe I can, sire."

"I *know* you can. I have not been idle since we met this morning. I have learned what I can about you both. I know how you turned Alexx's fortunes around, even though his wife squandered them. I know what you did for the prison camp. Now I'm confident of what you can do for me. So, Glennall, say yes and get on with the work you must do," the king concluded.

"Then: yes, sire."

"Good," King Akvych affirmed. Next, he looked at James. "And as for you …"

"I'll be his assistant," James said dryly.

This time the king was surprised. "How did you know?"

James smiled. "I'm *always* his assistant. I think it's what I was sent here to do."

That night, James was amused to watch as Glennall was fitted for an entirely new wardrobe. The servants fluttered around him, taking measurements, trying different colors, making him stand this way or stretch his arms out that way.

The whole time, James sat and observed while eating from a bowl of grapes. "You haven't told the king who you are," he said when the servants had gone.

Glennall glanced uneasily around him, making sure no one could overhear. "I don't intend to," he replied.

"Why not?"

"Why should I? It would serve little purpose."

James had to agree. If the king found out that Glennall was from a wealthy family in Marus, he might suspect him of being a spy or of giving away their plans for the future or …

"I'm going to change my name so my family won't realize who I am."

"Change it to what?"

"Simply *Glenn*."

"They won't know?"

"It's a common name in both Marus and Palatia." He rubbed his chin. "I think I'll also grow a beard."

"Can you?"

"Of course I can." Then an odd smile crept onto Glennall's face.

"What's so funny?" James asked.

"My family."

"What about them?"

"If only they could see me now." Glennall laughed long and hard at the thought. But James detected a hint of darkness in his eyes, an edge to his laugh.

"You've given up on the idea of revenge, I hope."

He looked at James with a frown. "Given up? When the Unseen One has put me in a position to make things right with my brothers—to *show* them? No, I have not given up."

James popped another grape into his mouth. "What's the point?"

"The point? The point is that they betrayed me and I will get back at them for it. Why else would the Unseen One put me in this position?"

"Maybe so you can do *other* things," James said. "A lot has happened since the cave. Everything has turned out so well. I don't understand why you want to hurt them."

"You can't understand. It's impossible for you to understand."

James began to feel hot under the collar. "Why is it *impossible* for me to understand? Look, Mr. Big Shot, everything that's happened to you has happened to me, too. I was kidnapped and sold as a slave just like you were. I wound up in the prison camp just like you did. I was beaten and pushed around just like you. It's not like you suffered anything by yourself."

"But you weren't abandoned by your family."

"Wasn't I?" James challenged, the emotion rising in his throat as he thought of his parents and how they left him behind—how they died.

Glennall was too lost in the argument to realize how James was feeling. He replied defensively, "You were abandoned in a manner of speaking, yes, but not like *I* was abandoned. I was my father's favorite. I was destined to be the *leader* of my family. I was going to be a rich and powerful ruler in my country. Whereas *you*—" Glennall stopped himself, blushing furiously.

"Whereas I *what?*" James demanded, standing up and spilling the bowl of grapes.

"I mean—"

"I wasn't going to be anybody, is that what you were going to say? I'm just an orphan, some tramp you took under your wing. Now I get it. I see what you really think about me." James stormed out of the room, nearly knocking a servant over in the hallway on the way to his own room. He slammed the door and threw himself on the bed.

Growling, he lay there with clenched fists, feeling as if steam were rising from his body. *The nerve!* he thought. *He's too big for his britches now and doesn't need me anymore.*

Footsteps fell past the door. He wondered if Glennall would come in to apologize.

Then came the doubt. Why should Glennall apologize? For hurting his feelings or speaking the truth? James wasn't the son of a wealthy man. He was an orphan, there was no denying it. And he hadn't accomplished anything on his own. Everything he'd done in this world had been with Glennall—*because* of Glennall. It was Glennall's brains that got them into such a good position with Alexx. The same was true at the prison camp. What had James done? Not much. And now all he had to look forward to was wandering around the countryside on Glennall's coattails.

What am I doing here? he wondered. Maybe his purpose for coming to this world had been fulfilled: He had somehow helped Glennall get to the top position in the land. Surely that's why the Unseen One had brought him here. There was nothing else for James to do.

It's time to go home, he thought.

CHAPTER SIXTEEN

———◆———◆———

James turned the knob in the wall near the head of the bed. Nearly 10 minutes later a servant came, looking as if he'd just awakened and had hastily dressed to answer James's call.

Embarrassed, James realized it was after midnight. "I need to talk to Chalcer," he told the servant.

"Can it wait until morning?" the servant replied.

"I won't be here in the morning."

The servant looked surprised, then hurried off. Five minutes later, a different servant returned and said, "Follow me."

Chalcer was alone in what they called the Games Room. It was a large room with tables for playing billiards, table tennis, even cards. Chalcer, dressed casually, was hunched over a billiard table with a cue, setting up a shot.

"Come in," he invited James. The balls clacked as he took his shot. "Do you play?"

"No, sir."

"I could teach you."

"No, thank you."

Chalcer moved around the table to take another shot. "They said you want to leave us."

"Yes, sir."

"Why?"

"I think I've done all I can do here. It's time to go home."

Chalcer took his shot, grunted at the result, then took another position on the table. He said, "I was also told that you and Glennall had an argument."

James shrugged. "Not really."

137

"They said you got angry and rushed out of the room." He took another shot, clacking more balls. "That sounds like an argument to me."

"I was mad, yes, but that's beside the point. Glennall can do what he needs to do without me. It's time for me to go home."

"Where is home?"

"It's …" James hesitated. He didn't know how to answer. "It's back through Marus."

Chalcer scanned the table as if he didn't know what shot to take next. "I think you should talk to Glennall first," he suggested after making up his mind.

"I'd rather not. He'd talk me into staying when I know I shouldn't. It's time to go."

Chalcer lined up his shot and took it. "Why tell me?" He stood up straight, putting chalk to the cue tip.

"Because you can tell the guards not to stop me."

"Aren't you afraid of being picked up as a runaway slave?"

James had forgotten that, technically, he was still a slave. He didn't feel like one. And the king had said he would set them free. "I won't be if the king will set me free."

Chalcer took another shot, then stood up to face James. Shadows from hanging lamps flickered across his stocky body and sturdy face. "He already has."

James wasn't sure of what he'd just heard. "What?"

"He gave me the papers tonight. You and Glennall are free men again. I was going to tell you both tomorrow morning."

James was speechless. Finally he muttered, "Thank you."

"What are you planning to do, *walk* back to Marus?"

"I guess so."

"What'll you do for food on the way?"

"I don't know."

"Lodging?"

"I don't know."

"Do you even know how to get there?"

"No. But I'll bet I can figure it out."

Chalcer chuckled. "Are you normally so ill-prepared when you run away?"

James thought about all the times he had run away from Aunt Edna. "Yeah, I guess so."

Chalcer leaned over the table again and took another shot. Satisfied that the balls had gone where he wanted them to, he stood up again. "Allow me to make arrangements for you. You have done a great service for the king. I believe he would insist. Go back to your room and I'll send someone to you with the details."

"Thanks," James said. He went to the door, then paused there. "You won't tell Glennall?"

"I'll have to tell him something."

James thought about it a moment. "Tell him I went home. He'll understand."

The servant led James back to his room. About a half hour later, a knock came at the door. "Come in," James said.

Barric stepped in and announced, "You and I are going on a trip to Marus. I've got a couple of horses waiting outside."

"*You're* taking me?"

"I drew the short straw," he replied with a smile. "Have you packed your things?"

"I never had much."

They stepped into the hallway. James looked across at the door to Glennall's room.

"Are you sure you don't want to talk to him first?" Barric asked.

"I'm sure."

Somewhere near the border between Marus and Palatia, James wished he had walked. He had never ridden a horse before, and this first lesson was far more painful than he ever would have thought. By the time he and Barric stopped at an old, stony inn for breakfast, James figured his entire body was bruised and every muscle was strained.

"Where are we?" James asked after Barric helped him off the horse.

"Rockhaven," Barric replied. "It's a small village near the Valley of the Rocks."

A small, bald-headed man in an apron rushed out from the stable—a ramshackle structure of wood and tarpaper—to greet them. Barric instructed him to feed and water the horses. He led the horses away.

"Are you tired? Do you want to sleep?" Barric asked James. "This inn has rooms."

"I don't have any money," James admitted sheepishly.

Barric reached under his coat and produced a small, bulging purse. "You do now." He shook the bag, and the coins inside jingled. "With the king's warmest regards," he said as he opened it to show James the coins were all gold, then handed it over.

"The king is *giving* me this money?"

"More than just money," Barric explained, pulling an envelope from his coat pocket. "You are also to have this letter, sealed by the king himself, assuring your freedom and protection wherever you go. Even in Marus, it will be taken seriously. There is no one more powerful than King Akvych in all the surrounding countries."

"But why?" James asked as he held the purse and the letter.

Barric looked at James, perplexed by the question. "Why

not? From the moment you set foot in Palatia, you have served the king, whether you realized it or not. You assisted Alexx, you reformed one of our prisons, and you have given the king clear guidance toward the future. This is how he shows his gratitude."

James hired two rooms for himself and Barric. They had a large breakfast, then slept for a few hours. Resuming their journey that afternoon, they continued along the southern roads of Marus with the hope of being in Dremat later that night.

Of course, it took longer than they expected because of James's lack of skill with his horse.

It was late when they reached Dremat, but the town still seemed bright and active. It reminded James of a cross between a large town in a Western movie and an English village he'd seen in a geography book. There were wooden buildings filled with stores of groceries, clothes, hardware, and supplies. Nearby were buildings of stone or brick that had offices for lawyers, doctors, and dentists. Saloons and hotels were scattered up and down the main avenue.

On the far end of one street sat a small inn. Barric secured them a couple of rooms. James had a hot bath to try to soothe his aching body, and, after a meal of soup and bread, they went to bed.

"Where are we going now?" Barric asked once they'd risen, eaten breakfast, and retrieved their horses from the local stable.

This was the moment James had dreaded. "I'm not sure," he admitted.

Puzzled, Barric gazed at him. "You don't know where your home is?"

"I know *where* it is," James stammered. "I mean, in the sense that I know it's called Odyssey and where to go once I reach it. But I don't know exactly how to get there from here."

Barric stared at him blankly. "I don't understand a word you just said."

"I'll explain while we ride," James offered.

And he did. All the way up the side of one mountain and down another, he told his entire story to Barric—everything except Glennall's true identity. As they traveled, he searched for any clues, any familiar sights, that might remind him of where he first met Fantya, Visyn, and Deydra.

"It's a remarkable story," Barric finally said. They had stopped by a river to give the horses a drink and a rest.

"I wouldn't believe it if I were in your place."

"Why shouldn't I believe it?" Barric asked. "You and Glennall have some rather magical powers, powers I never thought were possible. I've never seen anyone with two colors of eyes like yours. So why would it be hard for me to believe that you came to this world from another?"

James didn't have an answer.

"Besides," he continued, "it doesn't matter whether I believe you or not. My assignment is to take you where you want to go. If it's a field in the middle of nowhere, then so be it. As long as I don't have to take you *all the way* into your world, I'm happy."

They stretched out under a large oak tree. It was a glorious summer day. The sun seemed to warm and massage James's aching limbs. The birds sang sweetly in the treetops and lulled him to sleep.

CHAPTER SEVENTEEN

James didn't know how long he'd been asleep—a few minutes, maybe an hour—but suddenly someone shouted, and it startled him awake. He sat up. Barric was on his feet, his body tense and poised as if he were about to pounce on something. Then James noticed there were maybe a dozen rough-looking men surrounding them. Two or three had muskets. With their homemade clothes, wild hair, and beards, they had the look of frontiersmen.

"We are unarmed," Barric said.

"You're trespassing," one of the men growled. His demeanor made James think he must be their leader.

James stood up. The sun was in his eyes, so he shielded them with his hand.

Barric spread his arms. "How were we to know? We saw no signs. No one warned us."

"Everybody around here knows that this land belongs to Connam and his sons."

"My king knows Connam," Barric said. "And until now, we've always had free passage through these lands."

"Who is your king?" the leader asked.

"King Akvych of Palatia."

"You are here on a mission for him?"

"Indirectly, yes."

"Then you'll want to speak with our master."

"You'll take me to Connam?"

"No, to his beloved son Sesta." The leader waved his hand at them. "Get your horses and come along with us."

143

The band of men guided James and Barric along winding lanes through the forest. Eventually they reached a large, wooden gate that took them to a clearing. In the center stood a big, timbered house with stairs leading up to a porch that encompassed all sides. It had elaborate gables, shuttered windows, and a tower that stuck up arrowlike out of the main building. The house was not ornate or majestic in the way so many of the Palatian manors was, but it had a wealthy simplicity.

A large man with a bushy beard was on the porch near the front door, giving instructions to a group of men. They acknowledged whatever he said and took off in another direction. He had turned to go back inside when he spied the band of men bringing James and Barric. He waited where he stood. James knew him at once: Sesta.

"We found them by the river," the leader shouted as they approached. "The older one claims to be from King Akvych."

"King Akvych has sent a messenger to me?" Sesta asked. "Bring them up."

Two of the men took the reins to the horses from Barric and James and led the animals away. Escorted by half a dozen of the other men, Barric mounted the steps with James following.

Sesta had sat down on a lounge chair and beckoned his guests to sit as well.

"I bring greetings from King Akvych," Barric said formally after taking a seat.

"The king and his representatives are always welcome here," Sesta said. His eyes moved from Barric to James, then stopped on James's face. At first James thought Sesta had recognized him from that day with Nosz. Then he realized it wasn't recognition but fear that spread across Sesta's face. Sesta was staring at James's eyes.

"Leave us," Sesta commanded his men.

The leader looked puzzled. "What?"

Sesta turned on him. "Go! Leave us alone."

The leader muttered to the men, and they marched off.

"Who are you, and what do you want?" Sesta asked. His tone had changed. It no longer had the formal politeness he'd used with Barric but was now hard and threatened.

"I have brought this young man back to Marus," Barric began to explain.

Sesta cut him off. "What business does the king of Palatia have with a prophet of the Unseen One?"

"Prophet?"

"Don't you see? He has the mark of the Unseen One."

"Ah, his different-colored eyes," Barric replied. "Palatians aren't superstitious about such things. This young man has been of service to the king, and, as a favor, we're bringing him back to his homeland."

"Then why bring him to me?" Sesta asked.

"Because he asked to be brought here."

"He doesn't belong here," Sesta said sharply. He was staring at James again. "Take him somewhere else. He's from the Unseen One, which usually means nothing but trouble for me and my family. He's a sign, an omen, that something terrible is about to happen to us."

"Something bad is going to happen, but it won't be my fault," James said, speaking for the first time.

"You see?" Sesta spat at Barric. "Take him back to Palatia. I don't want anything to do with the boy."

"I don't want to go back to Palatia," James stated simply. And suddenly he knew that it wasn't only because of Glennall. He didn't want to go back because he was *supposed* to be in Marus. It was a certainty that surprised him. Was the Unseen One at work again?

"Then go somewhere else."

Barric stood up. It was clear to him that nothing remained to be discussed. "Let's be on our way, James."

But James knew he wasn't supposed to go. He was supposed to be here now. Why, he couldn't say. But he knew it was true, so he said the only thing he could think of to get Sesta to back down: "How are your brothers?"

"My brothers?"

"You have brothers."

"Ten of them." Sesta eyed him suspiciously.

"But you had 11."

Sesta nodded. "It's common knowledge that one of our beloved brothers was tragically killed by wild animals."

"Wild animals?" James asked carefully. "I thought he'd fallen down a mine shaft."

Sesta looked at James, a suspicious look on his face. "Wild animals killed him in the forest. We never found the body, but we found his bloodstained clothes."

James kept his eyes on Sesta. "Did anyone look in the mines for his body? In Arinshill Mine, for example?"

Sesta didn't answer.

Confused by this exchange, Barric suggested impatiently, "James, if we're returning to Palatia, we should leave now."

"Shall I leave for Palatia?" James asked Sesta coolly.

Sesta stared back, as if trying to read James's intentions on his face. Then he suddenly said, "No. You are welcome here."

"You want him to stay?" Barric asked, surprised by this dramatic change of heart.

"Yes. Thank you."

Barric turned to James. "And do you want to stay?"

James simply nodded.

"Then I'll say good-bye."

Sesta called for one of his men to bring the horses around.

James walked with Barric down the steps to the waiting horses and shook his hand. "Thank you for everything, Barric," he said warmly. "You've been a real pal."

Leaning close to James, Barric whispered, "Remember the letter. I don't trust this man, nor should you."

"I'll watch my step."

Barric smiled and mounted his horse. He took the reins of the second horse and tied them to the horn of his saddle. "Until we meet again," he said.

"Do you think we will?" James asked.

"I hope so." Barric nudged his horse and rode off toward the gate and his journey home.

After Barric had disappeared around the bend, Sesta stepped up to James and asked, "What am I to do with you?"

"I had hoped to go home, but now ..."

"Tell me where it is and I will have my men take you immediately," he offered, sounding almost desperate. "The sooner I can be rid of you, the better."

"Why? I haven't done anything to you."

"But you will," he said despondently. "I know the stories of the prophets. I know how the Unseen One punishes those who displease Him. You're like a dark thundercloud that hides a fury of lightning. If I were my former self, I would strike you down here and now to keep your mouth closed."

"Like you did your brother?"

Sesta's face hardened, but his hands trembled. "I won't argue with what you know or don't know about him. All I can say is that I have learned a lot since he *disappeared*. I am not the man I was. I see now that I have made terrible mistakes. But I cannot undo them. My brothers and I carry on as peacefully as we can."

"What about your father?"

"Don't toy with me, boy. If you know more than you're saying, speak plainly."

"Is he alive?"

"He is alive in his body, but his heart died the day we told him of our brother's disappearance. We had no idea how much he loved Glennall." Sesta looked away. James thought the man might cry. But after a moment, he turned back to James, steely-eyed. "What do you want from me?"

James couldn't answer. Though he was sure about staying here, he didn't know why or what he should do next.

"Well?" Sesta demanded.

"There was a man," James began slowly, trying to remember. "He knows about the Unseen One. He was a priest."

"Brother Dilliam."

"That's him." James remembered the name from Glennall. "He lives at the shelter, farther up the mountain."

"A shelter?"

"It's a small community of fanatics," Sesta said derisively. "Men like him who live and breathe the Unseen One."

"Kind of like a monastery."

"If I knew what a monastery was, I might agree. As it is, I'm sure he'll make you feel welcome there."

"Then please take me to him."

The trip up the mountain was difficult for James, not because the traveling was difficult but because he still didn't trust Sesta. Even with Sesta's little speech about being a changed man, James suspected there were still a lot of mine shafts left to be thrown into. He braced himself to run like a rabbit at the first sign of trouble.

James was relieved but exhausted when they reached the iron door of what looked like a small fort. Sesta pulled a rope, and somewhere beyond the high, wooden walls, a bell rang. A moment later, the iron door opened, the hinges groaning from its weight. A tiny, white-haired man—even smaller than James—peered out at them.

"Tell Dilliam that Sesta has brought him a guest," Sesta ordered.

The man, dressed in a tunic, rushed off.

"I hope you enjoy it here," Sesta told James, then started off with his men. "Dilliam will know what to do with you."

James felt a sick feeling in his stomach, as if he'd made the biggest mistake of his life. Maybe he should have stayed with Barric. For that matter, maybe he should have stayed with Glennall in Palatia. He was safe there. Now he felt as if he were about to be sold into slavery again. He thought quickly, *If I run now, I can still go back to Palatia.*

"Ah!" someone exclaimed. James turned toward the sound of the voice at the door and found himself looking up at a giant of a man. He must have been well over six feet tall, with a crown of thin, red hair that seemed spun around his face. His eyes were framed between the roundness of his cheeks and his forehead, but they sparkled anyway. He had a large mouth, framed by a red beard, that stretched into an enormous smile. He wore a long, brown tunic. "I've been expecting you," he said in a low rumble of a voice.

Any fear or apprehension James had felt now melted in the brightness of this man. He was a complete stranger to James, yet James felt as if he'd known him all his life. *This is where I'm supposed to be*, James thought.

"Yes," the man said, his tone a warm blanket of comfort. "This is where you're supposed to be."

CHAPTER EIGHTEEN

"This is your room," the man said.

James had followed the giant from the front door and across a courtyard filled with flowers of more colors than he thought possible—all of them more rich and vibrant than James had ever seen—with a well in the middle. They went to a long, single-story building off to the right. The man had to stoop to enter. The building had a hall stretching its length and many small rooms on both sides. The giant opened one of the doors in the middle of the hall and gestured for James to enter.

"Thank you," James said as he stepped into the small, square room. It had a window, a single bed, a wooden bedside table, a dresser with two drawers, and a trunk.

"We keep extra blankets in the trunk," the man explained.

"Who are you?" James asked.

"I am Brother Dilliam."

"I thought so," James responded. "Why did you say you were expecting me?"

"Because it's true. We've been expecting you for quite a while now. We have seen it in our writings and heard whispers of it in our prayers."

"About *me?*"

Dilliam smiled. "You have been sent by the Unseen One."

James saw in Dilliam's eyes a deep sympathy, a compassion. For the first time, he felt he'd finally met someone who could help him understand what was going on. "Why? Why has the Unseen One sent me here?"

"Let's find out together," Dilliam replied.

James suddenly felt very tired. He sat down on the edge of the bed. The mattress was thick and comfortable.

"You rest now," Dilliam suggested. "We have plenty of time to talk in the days and months ahead."

"Days and months?" James asked, yawning. "I don't think we have that long. Trouble is coming."

Dilliam began to pull the door closed. "Rest first and then we'll talk."

James rolled back onto the mattress. It was so soft that he felt as if he had climbed onto a cloud. He fell asleep quickly, a deep and dreamless sleep, and didn't awaken until after dark. When he got up, two of the monks—he assumed they were monks because of their brown tunics—stood at the door with lamps. They seemed startled by his waking and quickly retreated.

The small, white-haired man who'd first answered the door now entered with a lamp. He set it on the bedside table. "You'll have to forgive them," he apologized. "Everyone is very curious to see you."

"I'm nothing special," James said.

"On the contrary, we are *all* special in the eyes of the Unseen One. But your gifts set you apart from the rest of us, so, naturally, our humanity responds with feelings of curiosity and wonder."

James had no idea what the man was talking about. "What's your name?"

"I'm Brother Jessup," he replied.

"I'm James."

"I know." Brother Jessup returned to the door. "I have laid out a tunic for you. Brother Dilliam thinks you'll be more comfortable in it than in your city clothes. Then, when you're ready, we'll be eating supper in the kitchen. It is in the building directly across from this one."

James wanted to ask more questions, but Brother Jessup left before he could. He slowly got up and changed into the tunic. Brother Dilliam was right. It was more comfortable than his other clothes. He then ventured to the kitchen.

"Come in and sit with us," Brother Dilliam invited from the head of a long, wooden table. It sat in the middle of the kitchen. About two dozen brothers stood on both sides of it, as if they were waiting for James. The only empty chair was next to Brother Dilliam, so James took it.

"Have mercy upon us," Dilliam intoned.

"Have mercy," the brothers repeated.

"For this food we are grateful."

Everyone sat down and began to eat. Though the various brothers chatted among themselves, James was aware that they kept watching him out of the corner of their eyes.

"We have a set routine here," Brother Dilliam told James. "We share in all the responsibilities and chores, taking equal turns in the garden, in the kitchen, in cleaning the rooms, in whatever must be done to maintain our community. You will take your part with us in the morning."

"I still don't know what I'm doing here," James whispered, embarrassed.

Dilliam whispered back, "You will, my son. There is much we will all learn from the work of our hands—and of our hearts."

After the meal, they all went to another part of the building that had a chapel with pews facing an altar. There they read a story from a large scroll about the Unseen One and how He had first spoken to a man called Marus, for whom their nation was named. Then they sang songs James had never heard before. Brother Dilliam spoke for a few moments about the ways of the Unseen One and His never-ending love and mercy as shown to the people in good times and bad. He spoke of faith in the Unseen One even when we don't understand His ways. He spoke of service to the Unseen One even when we have nothing to gain from it. After that, they spent time in silent prayer.

James still didn't understand the Unseen One very well, but he felt a feeling of peace wash over him like a gentle summer shower. He wanted to stop time and hold this moment forever.

The service ended, and Dilliam invited James to walk with him in the garden. The smells of the flowers filled James's head, and the warmth of the summer night made him feel contented.

"I could stay here forever," James said abruptly, surprising himself with the statement.

"That's how many people feel when they first come," Dilliam replied. "But after a while, they get restless and move on." He spoke without reproach or disappointment. He said it all as a statement of fact. "This life, the life of the brothers, is only for those chosen by the Unseen One to live it."

"Then I've been chosen for it. I've never felt this ... this *good*."

"I'm glad you do. For this is the time of joyous preparation. Enjoy it while you can."

"Preparation for what?"

"For the difficulties to come ... and for your part in them."

"What difficulties?"

"There will be financial ruin for all who depend on such things. And then the livestock and the crops will suffer from mysterious diseases. Many will face starvation."

James's mouth fell open. "You *know* about that?"

"Yes. It was revealed to us by the Unseen One."

"But what does it have to do with me?"

"Your part is to help save the people of Marus."

James shook his head. "You've got it all wrong. I'm not going to save anybody. It's Glennall who's—"

Dilliam put his hand to his lips suddenly, as if masking his astonishment.

James instantly felt foolish. It was his intention never to mention Glennall's name. If Glennall's family or any of the people in Marus knew that Connam's son was alive in Palatia, and not only alive but wielding great power, it could complicate things for everyone.

"Then Glennall is alive, as I have always believed," Dilliam said thoughtfully.

James didn't answer at first.

"Tell me all, son," Dilliam encouraged him.

James resisted. He thought he shouldn't tell. But as he looked up at Dilliam, his resolve broke. If ever there was someone who could hear all and make sense of it, Dilliam was the one. James told him everything, from the point when he ran away from Aunt Edna to the point when he was standing at the shelter's door with Sesta. Dilliam listened attentively, interrupting once or twice to ask a clarifying question, and then nodded appreciatively when James had finished.

"Your secret is safe," Dilliam said as he put a reassuring hand on James's shoulder. "But it gives me an important piece to the puzzle. All our studying and praying told us that our hope for Marus in the time ahead would come from the south, from Palatia, but we couldn't imagine how Palatia would ever help us in a time of need. Traditionally, they befriend us only when we have something to offer them. Otherwise, they hope for our downfall. But if Glennall is there ..." Dilliam stroked his beard absentmindedly.

"He's there, all right," James said. "And he's in a position to help everyone. You'll see. That's why I think you've got it wrong. Glennall will take care of everything. I'm just a ... a nobody."

"That's where *you* are wrong, my son," Dilliam said kindly. "You have been brought from your world for more than you know. But you can only understand as time goes on."

The time did go on in a daily routine as consistent as a ticking clock. James spent his early mornings milking the three cows, feeding the chickens, and taking care of the goats and sheep. He and the other brothers then met in the chapel, learning the stories of the Unseen One from countless scrolls, and singing and praying. Next he helped Brother Jessup and the other brothers with breakfast and chores around the kitchen. From there they tended the gardens, cultivating flowers and growing vegetables. They took great care as well with a small orchard of fruit trees to the rear of the grounds.

A break in the afternoon allowed for rest or recreation. Often, during that time, Dilliam or Brother Jessup would tutor James in subjects like math and science and the arts. After that, their various assigned chores continued until dinnertime. Everyone helped with the cooking and washing up. Then came the evening service of songs and prayer, another time of relaxation and conversation, and finally bed. In the morning, it began all over again.

One day each week, the brothers were free simply to enjoy themselves. James went fishing in a nearby stream with Brother Jessup, wandered the forest close to the shelter (he was warned to stay clear of the timber mills and the mines or anything to do with Connam's family), or relaxed in the garden and read.

James understood how a lot of people might find that kind of life tedious or boring. *He* would've thought so before he'd come to Marus. But now he didn't. The kindness and love of the brothers, especially Brother Dilliam, made him feel happier and more contented than he ever had.

He also enjoyed studying more than he thought possible. The stories of the Unseen One held him spellbound. He read about the creation of the world through the Unseen One; the rise and fall and rise again of the first human beings; the many stories of Marus, who at first rejected the Unseen One and then became the father figure of the entire nation; and the events leading up to the Great Catastrophe, when a mysterious young boy, a messenger from another world, became the Unseen One's means of judgment against a sinful and rebellious world.

Through these stories, and through the daily show of love from the brothers, James came to realize that he had completely misunderstood the Unseen One. He was certainly a far cry from the deity James had heard about through Glennall. James had been given the impression that the Unseen One was powerful and calculating, moving people around like pieces on a chessboard. That's why he and Glennall had been given the visions—so they could rise through the ranks at Alexx's, at the prison camp, and with the king. Now Glennall had all the power he could ever want, and he would use it to get back at his brothers. The Unseen One had made it all possible in order to "set things right" (as Glennall had kept saying).

"It's all part of the mystery," Dilliam explained when James brought up his confusion. "The purposes of the Unseen One are being realized even while Glennall pursues his own purposes. They seem to be intertwined, and yet they're not. Not as we think. Ultimately, the purposes of the Unseen One will overcome all other purposes, to the extent that, in the end, we may look back and think that all we said and did was according to His plan all along, like actors in a play."

James shook his head. "It makes no sense to me."

Dilliam smiled. "Nor to me. But such is the tension between our purposes and His. All we can hope to do is to fulfill our roles to the best of our abilities."

"What role am I playing?" James asked.

Dilliam gazed at James intently. "I believe you are the hinge on which the door swings."

"What?"

"You will make it possible for the people to be saved."

"I don't get it," James confessed. "How?"

Dilliam held up a cautioning hand. "You'll know when it happens."

James frowned. "Do they teach you guys how to be mysterious in a school somewhere? Why can't everyone just come right out and say what they mean?"

Dilliam laughed heartily. The walls seemed to shake from it. Then he replied, "Because we don't know the full answers ourselves. If all I have is a distant picture, a distant picture is all I can describe to you."

James pondered Dilliam's words in the days and weeks that followed. Summer turned to autumn, and the world began to change outside the walls of the shelter. The trouble began.

James noticed it first in the growing number of beggars who stopped by the shelter for food or a place to sleep. Where before they had only one or two a week, that increased to several a day, and then more.

Some of the beggars told sad stories of how their businesses had gone bust. The nation's money was running out, they said, because the rich leaders had spent it on bad ideas. People were slowly being driven out of their jobs and then their homes.

James had heard also that the Connam family had had to close down some of the mills and mines because times were so bad. He shuddered as he remembered how the same things had happened in his world as a trigger for the Depression.

James heard stories about Palatia, too. The beggars told how King Akvych had found a shrewd young man called Glenn who was leading their country into prosperity. Some said they thought he had the magic of telling the future, as if he *knew* the crisis was coming. He was forcing the people of Palatia to ration their provisions, creating laws to make them put some of it aside in royal storehouses. This was a scandal, since the Palatians didn't think the economic problems in other countries would ever reach them. But the king insisted, even bringing out his army to enforce the law.

Then, in the middle of the harvest, a blight attacked the crops. It was a disease no one had ever seen before. All the crops simply dried up and died, turning to a brittle dust that blew away in the slightest breeze. The rumor was that it had begun in the north, in the country of Albany, then spread west into Adria, then south into Gotthard and Marus and onward into Palatia.

Things went from bad to worse when a plague hit the livestock. It reminded James of rabies, though no one in Marus had ever heard of such a thing. No animals were excluded, and those that didn't die were so diseased as to be useless for food. People who dared to eat the meat wound up getting the disease themselves.

Fish seemed to be the only thing left to eat, but there weren't enough in the streams and rivers to feed all the people. Territorial wars broke out on the Androclyne Sea, which formed the eastern borders of Albany, Marus, and Palatia, as each country fought for what fish could be found there.

To everyone's horror, the fish, though healthy enough, began to make people ill with terrible stomach cramps. Some people died.

Many of the older people in Marus said it was the Great Catastrophe all over again. "It is the wrath of the Unseen One!" they cried. They prayed as they had never prayed before. Panic seized the surrounding countries. People began to starve.

The shelter itself seemed untouched by the problems. The brothers had always been self-sufficient, and, since their livestock didn't get sick and their fruit and vegetables grew without disease, they could continue as before. Brother Dilliam declared that it was the mercy of the Unseen One that saved them, and that His mercy should not go unshared. So the brothers all agreed to ration the food to themselves so there would be more to give to the poor and hungry who came to them.

One day in early October, the bell for the door rang once again. No one else was about, so James rushed to answer it.

"Please, sir—" a young woman began, then stopped herself with a sharp gasp, her eyes big as saucers. "You!"

"Fantya?" James exclaimed.

Without hesitation, they embraced like long-lost friends.

"I thought you were gone forever," she said. "A slave ... or perhaps dead!"

James gestured for her to come inside. "Please. We have food."

"I'm not a beggar," she said proudly.

"I didn't say you were," James countered. But he noticed her thin face, protruding cheekbones, and recessed, dark eyes beneath the dark hair that still spread wildly from her head. Her peasant dress was also the same, but it looked the worse for wear. Her family had been affected by the hard times. But James still thought she was the prettiest girl he'd ever seen. "I'm asking you to come in as my guest. Where are your mother and father?"

"My father is in Dremat, seeking what little business he can find."

"And your mother?"

"She is dead," the girl replied in a flat tone.

"I'm sorry."

"She was never in the best of health. And these times are so … so difficult … that she didn't have the strength to survive."

"Come in." James took her arm and led her into the shelter. As they walked to the kitchen, he asked, "What are you doing up here if your father is Dremat?"

"He has asked me to find Nosz."

"Nosz! Here?"

"He still does business with Connam's sons—mostly with Sesta. We were told he was on the mountain even now."

"Why in the world would you want to talk to him?"

"Because, though we're not starving now, we will starve. My father wants to beg Nosz's help to find business with the Connam family. We have nothing left. It's our only hope."

"You're Palatians," James said in obvious confusion. "I thought everyone in Palatia was doing well because of the king's man."

"Glenn?" she suddenly spat. "Glenn is no friend to the people of Palatia. Oh, he was helpful at first, but now he's using the hard times to profit the king."

"What do you mean?"

"He announced that he would ration back to us the food and provisions he has been keeping in store—in exchange for our land and property."

"Glennall is using the crisis to buy up real estate?"

"He's a clever young man," Fantya said with a scowl. "Buy it all up now, and then when the crisis is over, the king will own everything. Those who give in will become nothing more than tenant farmers."

"But that isn't why he was put in charge!" James complained. "He was put in charge to *help* the people, not use their starvation against them! What in the world is he thinking?"

"You speak as if you know him."

James bit his tongue. "I ... I just don't like what he's doing, that's all."

They had reached the kitchen now, and James set about fixing food for her. One of the brothers spied them coming and raced away. James suspected he would rush to Brother Dilliam to say that a pretty girl had entered the shelter and was in James's company.

James assembled some fruit and vegetables. Fantya restrained herself as best as she could, but her hands quivered while she ate. James wondered how long it had been since she'd had her last meal. His heart went out to her.

"Tell me about what happened to you," she asked James between bites.

James told her his story, but in a way that made it sound as if he'd somehow escaped from Palatia and taken refuge in the shelter. He didn't want her to know that Glennall and Glenn were the same person, nor that he had connections to the king himself. All his instincts said that it would cause trouble for her to know.

Brother Dilliam arrived shortly thereafter, but he never betrayed any concern about James being with this attractive young woman. Instead, he played the perfect host, offering Fantya all the hospitality the shelter could afford. Fantya politely refused. "I must return to my father," she insisted.

"Find him and come back," James offered. "You'll be safe here."

"No. We are Palatians first and foremost. We must make our own way."

James walked with her to the door. An evening chill had come. Dark clouds gathered overhead. James thought he felt a drop of rain on his cheek. Fantya drew her arms around herself, then suddenly leaned over and kissed James on the cheek. "Thank you for your kindness," she said warmly.

"Don't go to Nosz," James pleaded with her. "Don't make any deals with him. He's a nasty man. Brother Dilliam knows Connam personally. He can put in a good word for you."

Fantya replied gently, "I will speak with my father. But I can make no promises of what we'll do."

James needed more reassurance from her than that and put his hand on her arm to stop her from leaving. She looked him full in the face with her dark eyes. They defied him. Her pride would not allow her to accept anything else from him.

"Good-bye," she said and stepped onto the path outside the door.

The rain began to fall steadily. James watched her until she had become part of the rain and the forest itself. He felt sick at heart. *Why am I here?* he wondered. *I'm not helping anyone by hiding in this shelter.*

Brother Dilliam placed a hand on his shoulder.

"Close the door," he said. "When next we open it, we will open other things as well."

CHAPTER NINETEEN

"**W**hy don't I dream anymore?" James asked Dilliam the next morning. They were in the courtyard, clearing up the leaves that had blown in with the previous night's storm.

"You don't dream?"

"I don't have dreams like I did before—you know, dreams that show me things."

"I can't answer that question with any certainty. The Unseen One will do as He pleases," came the reply. "But you have to remember that dreams are not an end unto themselves. They're merely a *means* to an end. It's by the touch of dreams that the Unseen One nudges us in the direction He would like us to go. If you're no longer having dreams, perhaps it is because you are on the right path."

The bell for the door jingled somewhere overhead. Brother Jessup seemed to appear from nowhere and rushed to answer it. The visitor was a messenger from Connam. He wanted to speak with Brother Dilliam immediately.

"You will accompany me," Dilliam informed James.

Soon thereafter, they began their journey farther up the mountain to Connam's home. It was at least a two-hour walk, even longer this day because the path was slick with mud from the rain. After a while, James asked, "You knew this would happen, didn't you?"

Dilliam tilted his head slightly. "You may not be dreaming anymore, but I am."

"You dreamed that we would be called to Connam?"

"I dreamed that Connam would summon me, but I saw in my dream that you were to come with me. You're to accompany me wherever I go."

"But—"

"No questions, my son," Dilliam interrupted. "Let's discover the answers together."

Connam's home was a castle, plain and simple. It had a moat surrounding it and a drawbridge, towers, and turrets— all the things James would have expected to see on a castle. As they approached, Dilliam informed him that it had been built generations before on the very site where the noble Arin had once lived with his family, right after the Great Catastrophe.

Servants were hustling and bustling in the courtyard, on the terraces, and up and down the many corridors.

"Why the frenzied activity?" Dilliam asked one young servant.

The servant looked around quickly to make sure he wasn't being watched or overheard. "We are packing to leave. But ask me no more, sir," he replied and rushed off.

Connam was in his chamber, a large, simply furnished room. Colorful tapestries hung on the walls, but the rest of the room was made up of modest wooden tables and chairs. A large, square table occupied the middle of the room. Connam sat there, papers and scrolls, pens and inkwells spread out before him.

If this is where Glennall grew up, James thought, *I now understand why he thought the houses of Palatia were so gaudy.*

Connam stood up to welcome them. He was nearly as tall as Dilliam but looked older and frailer. He embraced Dilliam warmly, then hooked a shriveled thumb at James.

"Who is he?" the old man asked in a low, croaky voice.

"My apprentice," Dilliam replied.

Connam didn't look at James or pay much attention to him throughout the rest of the conversation. "You see the chaos of my house?" he asked, gesturing for Dilliam to sit down. James drifted over to a large, stone fireplace where a fire raged. The warmth of it was a comfort.

"Yes, my lord, I noticed the chaos," Dilliam answered.

"We are packing to go down the mountain."

"Who, my lord?"

"My entire family."

"Are times so bad for you?"

"Not yet, but they will be if we continue on our present course." Connam coughed, then continued. "We will all go to our family home near the Valley of the Rocks. I will wait there."

"Wait, my lord?" Dilliam inquired. "Wait for what?"

"For news of the success or failure of my sons' mission."

"You speak cryptically, my lord. I am a foolish man and do not understand."

"You are no fool," Connam stated, rapping a knuckle on the table to emphasize the statement. "All the families of Marus have asked me to go to Palatia to negotiate with the king's adviser."

"Glenn?"

"Yes. But I am too feeble to negotiate, so I am sending my sons—except the youngest—to negotiate on our behalf."

"What will you negotiate?"

"A treaty for food and supplies for our people."

Dilliam was surprised. "But you know the king's terms. He will only give food in exchange for land."

"Then we will give him land."

Dilliam's eyes widened. "You're prepared to give the king of Palatia access to the lands of Marus?"

"The land is no good to us if we starve to death," Connam replied, a hint of resignation in his voice.

"This is sobering news, my lord."

"So it is," Connam agreed. "But in the collective wisdom of the rulers of the nation, we could think of nothing else, no other action to take. Unless *you* can think of something. What would the Unseen One have us do?"

"I'm afraid the Unseen One has not advised me on the subject," Dilliam answered directly. "Humbly, though, while I can't affirm the decision to give Marutian lands to King Akvych, I *can* affirm your decision to have your sons meet with the king's adviser."

Has Dilliam lost his mind? James wondered. *To send Connam's sons to Glenn would put them right into Glennall's hopes for revenge. He might have them imprisoned on some ridiculous excuse: a charge of treason, spying, anything—or he might even have them killed.* James nearly spoke, the words catching in his throat as he stopped them. It sounded like a cough.

Dilliam shot him a warning glance.

"I'm glad you approve," Connam said, "because you're going with them."

"My lord?"

"I want you to go with my sons to Palatia."

"For what purpose, my lord?"

"To advise them." The old man took a deep breath, then leaned on his desk. "I have been a man of faith, as you know. I could fill the night telling of the adventures I have had with the Unseen One. Yet, at times I have behaved as if the Unseen One did not exist. It was the price of my success, I believe. Prosperity filled my purse while it robbed my soul."

"It is the way of men, my lord."

"So it is." Connam's eyes grew moist. "My beloved Glennall was the only one who sought the ways of the Unseen One. You taught him yourself."

"He was gifted, my lord."

"But I did not cherish his gifts as I should have. I didn't want him to grow up to be a priest. I wanted him to grow up to be a successful man of business. Like me. That was my heart's desire." Connam paused and wiped his eyes. "Now I would allow him to be anything, anything at all, if the Unseen One would return him to me alive." There was silence for a moment.

James kept his eyes away from the scene and stared at the yellow and red of the fire.

"We leave at daybreak, Dilliam. Make whatever plans you must through my servants. They will return to your shelter to gather whatever you need."

"I have few needs, my lord."

"Good."

"With your permission, I will bring my apprentice along. He is of great comfort to me."

"As you wish. My head steward will show you where you will sleep tonight. In the meantime, my home is your home. I may have need of your counsel later."

Dilliam signaled James that it was time to go and stood up. "I am at your service, my lord," he offered in parting. They left the room.

In the corridor, James opened his mouth to speak.

Dilliam held up a finger for him to stay silent. "No questions," he instructed.

The head steward approached and guided them to two rooms down a dark hallway in a quieter part of the castle. Dilliam drew up a list of things he wanted the servants to bring from the shelter, and he also gave them a note for Brother Jessup to explain what had happened.

James spent the rest of the day wandering around the castle, staying out of the servants' way, and trying to imagine what it was like for Glennall to grow up there. He visualized how difficult it must have been for Glennall to be so sickly and frail while his brothers were so strong and robust. On the other hand, it must have been galling for his brothers to have to play second fiddle to a weedy younger brother. And meanwhile, their father was oblivious to the hatred being bred between them, a hatred that would lead to betrayal and now maybe revenge.

As evening came, James had lost his way down one hallway and into a small corridor that led to several rooms. Frustrated that he didn't know where he was going, he paused at an open door to ask for help. He heard voices inside and waited for a moment to speak.

"You will obey me, my son!" It was Connam, his voice croaky but still commanding.

"I am humiliated," a young man replied. James guessed it was Transe, Glennall's younger brother, by their facial resemblance. "You allow all my brothers to go to Palatia but require me to stay with you. Will I never be able to cut your apron strings?"

"I will not lose you as I lost Glennall!" Connam insisted.

James didn't want to eavesdrop or be an unwelcome witness to their argument, so he quietly stepped away. It was too late.

"Why do you linger at my door?" Transe shouted.

James hadn't realized he'd been seen and stepped into the doorway, blushing. "I'm sorry," he apologized. "I lost my way and was trying to—"

"Who are you?" Transe demanded.

James was startled by Transe's anger and even more startled

by Transe's appearance. He looked so much like Glennall that it took James's breath away.

"He is Brother Dilliam's apprentice," Connam explained. "He's harmless."

Transe's tone softened. "I apologize for shouting at you. I'm sure one of the servants will help you if you go down the hall and turn left."

"Thank you," James replied and made to leave.

"Please close the door," Transe said.

James obeyed. As soon as the latch clicked, the shouting on the other side of the door resumed, with Connam pleading with his son to try to understand.

The entire family gathered in the castle's great hall for their evening meal. James finally got a closer look at the brothers he had only seen as ruffians that night at Arinshill Mine. It seemed like such a long time ago. But there they were, sitting on both sides of the table, eating bowls of a stew of some sort—a stew with more broth than meat or vegetables in it.

Sesta was clearly alarmed to see James and Dilliam there. He demanded to know why they had been joined by two *priests*, but Connam was firm in his answer and unyielding to any of Sesta's arguments. James was aware that Sesta watched him out of the corner of his eye for the rest of the meal.

James also recognized Rastall, the biggest and oldest, as the brother who didn't want Glennall killed. Drouse, a younger brother James recognized, also sided with Rastall at the mine. Besides Sesta and Transe (who pouted the entire night), the remaining seven men weren't familiar to James. They had been mostly shadows that night in his dream. And no matter how hard he tried during dinner, he couldn't match their names to their faces.

"Rastall is the oldest," Dilliam explained as they walked to their rooms much later.

"I know him."

"Then comes Sesta."

"I know him best of all."

Dilliam chuckled, "He must be wondering why you haven't told Connam what you know. It must be torture for him, though I'm sure he has come up with a ready means to denounce you if you ever speak against him."

"Which one is going bald?"

"That would be Turnan. And then there's Drouse."

"I recognized him."

"Then comes Naud, who had the scar on his cheek."

"Right."

"Followed by Yon. He wore the gold coat. He always wears gold coats."

"Okay."

"Then comes Cannap. He's the shortest of them all."

"Cannap is short. Got it."

"Then Fortawince, Pa'an, and Selsond."

"I'll never remember them."

"You probably won't have to."

James fell asleep while quizzing himself on the names of the brothers. He slept fitfully but figured it was because the castle was colder than he was used to.

The next morning, the horses and wagons were assembled in the courtyard, and everyone climbed on. Connam asked Brother Dilliam to say a prayer to the Unseen One, asking for a safe journey and successful visit to Palatia. Afterward, the procession slowly made its way from the castle and down the winding roads of the mountain.

It took three days to reach the family home near the village of Kellen, a little north of the Valley of the Rocks. Along the way, James saw multitudes of people heading toward Palatia. Most were thin and sick. They cleared the road for Connam's caravan, begging for food and water once they realized who was passing them. Dilliam and James gave what they could, but they were soundly rebuked by some of the brothers for giving away what wasn't their property.

Dilliam turned on the brothers and shouted, "Are you still not humbled by your lives and this downturn of your fortunes? Whatever you have, you have only because of the grace of the Unseen One. So do not rebuke me like selfish little boys."

None of the men spoke to him after that.

At Kellen, the wagons were unpacked, then reorganized for the next part of the journey to Muirk. Two brothers would drive each wagon, with Dilliam and James driving the smallest supply wagon in the rear. Great tension filled the air as the brothers argued over how to negotiate with Glenn. Some had resigned themselves to giving up most of their lands for food, while others wanted to drive a hard bargain in the hopes of getting the food without losing *any* lands.

It took another day to prepare for the trip to Muirk. When the drivers snapped the reins and the wagons lurched forward, James felt butterflies dancing in his stomach. He felt like an actor about to go on stage for the first time.

He sensed that the time had come for him to play his most-important part.

CHAPTER TWENTY

✦————————✦

Muirk was overrun with people. The streets were congested on all sides with travelers from every nation. The mix of voices and accents was a cacophony to James. The stench from so many animals and inadequate sanitation filled the air. The caravan seemed to move only inches at a time down the long avenue to the king's palace.

James felt a strange longing in his heart at the familiarity of this place. The memories came back to him of running errands for Glennall when they were in Alexx's household. But it was a clash of feelings, for he knew those streets as a slave, and he never wanted to be a slave again.

From his position on the wagon, James heard the name of Glenn spoken or whispered fearfully and apprehensively. And the closer they got to the king's palace, the more he dreaded what might happen. He didn't know who Glennall had become in the short time since they'd separated, but he figured he wouldn't like him.

The walls of the palace were in sight when Rastall commanded the caravan to pull to one side of the road. Sesta then leapt down from his wagon and disappeared into a tavern. A minute later, he returned with a large, barrel-chested man with a thick, dark beard.

"Nosz," James whispered to Dilliam.

Dilliam nodded appreciatively. "Will he recognize you?" he asked.

"I hope he does. I'd like to see the expression on his face."

"In the tavern," Nosz called to them. "I can give you news, but not here in the street."

The brothers, along with Dilliam and James, crowded into the small establishment. It had low beams that Dilliam knocked his head against once or twice. They found a long table and sat down. Nosz stood at the head of the table to address them.

He began, "I am gratified that you have entrusted me to—"

"Save your speeches for a banquet," Rastall commanded. "Have you met with Glenn on our behalf?"

Nosz lowered his head. "Not as such, no."

This caused an uproar among the brothers, who demanded an explanation.

"These things take time," Nosz tried to explain. As he spoke, his glance fell on James's face. He looked puzzled for a moment, as if he should know him from somewhere but couldn't remember where. He continued, "But I am pleased to say that I have an audience with Glenn *this afternoon*. I will not disappoint you."

"You'd better not," Sesta sneered.

"Meanwhile, you must remain here while I go," Nosz explained. "The accommodations are the best you'll find, under the circumstances." He moved around the table, quickly shaking the hands of the brothers as he went. When he reached Dilliam and James, he stopped.

"Do I know you, boy?" he asked softly.

"What did you do with Fantya?" James asked.

The question had its intended effect. Nosz looked as if someone had suddenly hit him with a club. He stammered for a moment, but no sensible words came. Finally he managed to say, "I have not seen her or her father."

Dilliam hooked a finger into the edge of Nosz's vest and

pulled him close. "Do not lie to us," he whispered. "She went to see you. What became of her?"

"I swear," he whispered back, his eyes darting nervously to the brothers. "She never came to me. I haven't seen her in months. Please, I must go to the palace." He wrenched free from Dilliam and left the tavern quickly without looking back.

James turned to Dilliam. "Do you believe him?" he asked.

"Yes, I do."

James breathed a sigh of relief. "Maybe she found another way to get help. As long as she stayed away from him, I'm happy."

They all waited at the tavern for the next two hours. The brothers continued to debate how they would approach Glenn. They also speculated about the man himself.

"They say he's wily and shrewd," said Naud, the one with the scar on his cheek.

"He'd have to be to rise to the top the way he has," Turnan observed. "He's been ruthless."

Fortawince added, "He didn't start out that way. Do you remember? We all thought that his forced rationing, before all the trouble started, was absurd. Now, of course, we see that he was a genius."

"Or a prophet," Rastall suggested moodily.

"A Palatian prophet?" Naud scoffed.

"What makes you think he's Palatian?" Rastall challenged. "I've heard a lot of rumors, and one describes him as a for-eigner. He may be from Marus, for all we know."

"Or a fanatic from the Unseen One," Sesta proposed, giving James and Dilliam a cold look.

Cannap stood up and moved down the table toward them. "A worthy thought. What do *our* prophets of the Unseen One think about Glenn?"

Dilliam thought for a moment, then replied, "He's a man, no more or less. A gifted man, to be sure, but no more than a man."

Cannap pointed a finger at James. "What do you say, boy? We've all noticed your eyes. We know what the legends say about your kind. Prophesy for us!" He laughed.

"Leave him alone!" Sesta snapped. "Don't taunt him. Don't even talk to him. He's trouble for us. He's a bad omen."

Dilliam gazed at Sesta and asked, "Is this what you've become, Sesta? Have you turned from faith to superstition?"

"If it were up to me, you wouldn't be here," Sesta answered. "I would have left both of you in Marus."

The tavern door opened, and all eyes turned expectantly. It wasn't Nosz, and the brothers relaxed. James didn't relax, though. He knew who had entered. It was Barric.

Barric saw James as well and showed only the smallest hint of surprise. He winked at him with a friendly smile and then strode into the center of the tavern. He announced formally, "Gentlemen, I come on behalf of the esteemed Glenn."

The brothers all sat up and took notice.

"You? Where's Nosz?" Sesta asked.

"Sadly, Nosz cannot help you."

"Why not?" Sesta demanded, rising from his seat.

"Because he has been arrested," Barric replied. "Unfortunately for him, the esteemed Glenn recognized him as a well-known spy, as well as a slave trader and all-round scoundrel."

Revenge, James thought. Glennall must have recognized who Nosz was. James then wondered about Fantya and hoped—*believed*—that she and her father were all right somewhere.

"We pray the esteemed Glenn will not hold Nosz's deeds

against us," Drouse said quickly. James noticed that no one actually defended Nosz.

Barric didn't respond to that but said, "Glenn would like to meet with you. He knows well the House of Connam and believes you have much to discuss."

The brothers were pleased with the news. The butterflies began to dance in James's stomach again.

"When may we meet with Glenn?" Rastall asked.

"Right now," Barric said. "You are to follow me to the palace."

"Now?" Rastall asked, suddenly dusting at his clothes. "We would prefer to be dressed more suitably for an audience with the king's adviser."

"Your appearance is of no consequence to him," Barric said. "He wants to see you now."

They quickly returned to their wagons. Barric led the way down the main street to the front gates that James remembered so well. Rather than going up the main driveway to the front door, though, they were taken on a different driveway that went around to the right of the palace. James wondered if they would have to go in through the servants' entrance.

They did.

"The servants' entrance?" Sesta complained as they all climbed down from the wagons. "What indignation is this?"

Barric was unfazed. "The king is meeting various heads of state in the front hall. Besides, this is the fastest way to Glenn's reception room."

The reception room seemed like a smaller version of the king's Throne Room. It had chairs lined up, facing one another, with a larger chair on a platform at the end. A red canopy stood over the chair, as if keeping away a sun that never entered the room. The brothers all chose their seats. Dilliam and James stood near the back to watch the proceedings. Barric waited by the main door.

Only a minute or so after they'd arrived, a door behind the platform opened, and a young man walked in. Without looking at them, he went directly to the chair on the podium and sat down. James's heart skipped a beat. It was Glennall, without doubt, but his hair was longer and curly, and he had a full beard. James thought that his brothers *must* recognize him. But with his hair and beard and robes of state and the way he sat in the shadow created by the canopy, his features were obscured. James knew his brothers didn't recognize him at all. Besides, their long-lost brother was the *last* person they would have expected to see in the palace.

He was unsmiling and stern in his tone. "I have met with your representative and dealt with him accordingly," he announced. "You should choose your comrades more carefully."

Rastall stood up nervously. "My lord, do not hold it against us," he pleaded. "We have known the man in business only and know nothing of his character."

"Oh?" Glennall challenged. "Can one engage a person in business without knowing that person's character? Surely how one conducts his business reveals his character. Unless, of course, you *choose* to be blind to that person's character."

He's toying with them, James thought.

"My lord speaks wisely," Rastall said diplomatically. "We will be wiser ourselves in the future."

"Who are you, and what do you want from me?" Glennall asked as if suddenly bored with their conversation.

"We are the sons of Connam, a great man of Marus, whom I am sure you know of."

"Why should I know of him?"

"Because he's the most-powerful man in our country."

"If he's so powerful, why has he sent you to me?"

"That we may speak business with you."

"Business? Am I to believe that the great and powerful Connam of Marus needs to speak business with me? More likely he has sent you to *spy* on Palatia."

"No, my lord!"

"He wants you to search out any weakness that may have been caused by the plagues and famine. Why else would he send so many of you?"

"No, my lord, it isn't so! If anything, we are here to show you *our* weakness by negotiating for food. Connam acknowledges your wisdom in these times of trouble. He has the highest respect for all you have done for Palatia. His hope was to honor you by sending, not only one representative, but all of his sons to stand before you."

"*All* of his sons? I had heard that Connam has 12 sons, yet I see only 10 of you here."

"It's true, my lord, we were 12. But one of our beloved brothers was tragically killed by a wild animal. And the other, our youngest, has remained at home with our father for safety's sake."

"Safety's sake? Was the journey so perilous? Do you fear Palatian outlaws?"

"No, my lord. I confess that our father is old and frail and fears unnecessarily that his youngest son may die tragically just as our other brother died."

Glennall stood up and said impatiently, "This is nothing but double-talk and lies! You say one thing, and yet the truth is another. You say your father wishes to honor me by sending *all* of his sons, and yet he withholds one. You are spies!"

The rest of the brothers could no longer restrain themselves. They each cried out that they were not spies. Two guards stepped forward, positioning themselves on each side of Glennall's platform. *It's all part of his revenge,* James knew. *Is this what he had planned all this time, or is he making it up as he goes along?*

Glennall sat down again and spoke calmly. "Then allow me to test the truth of your words. One of you may return to Marus to bring me the missing brother."

"My father will never permit it," Rastall argued sharply.

Glennall seemed aghast. "Will he save one son and risk losing 10 others?"

"What do you mean?" Sesta suddenly asked.

"The rest of you will be my personal guests in the royal dungeon until the missing brother is brought to me. You have a minute to decide." Glennall stood up again and disappeared through the rear door.

In a collective shout, the brothers began to argue with each other about what to do.

During the argument, James glanced at Dilliam. "He's got a lot of nerve," James said. "He knows I could expose him right now."

"To what end?" Dilliam asked. "He has the upper hand. You cannot challenge his power. It's his *heart* that must be challenged."

"Then what should we do?"

Dilliam shrugged. "We must be patient to see how this plays out."

Glennall returned after precisely one minute and stood in front of his chair.

The brothers conceded their defeat and decided that Selsond should be the one to ride to Marus, since he was the best horseman, and bring Transe back.

Satisfied, Glennall ordered, "Barric, see them safely con-ducted to the dungeon." Then he pointed to James and

Dilliam. "But not them. They do not have to join these spies. They are free to go."

Dilliam stood up straight, his hands clasped in front of him, and said, "My lord, I was entrusted by Connam himself to accompany these men *wherever* they go. If they are to stay in the dungeon, then we must stay in the dungeon as well."

James smiled to himself. Dilliam was pushing to see just how far Glennall would go.

"Suit yourself," Glennall said, then walked out.

The guards led them down various corridors to the rear of the palace, then up other corridors toward the front again. These were sections James had not seen in his short time as a palace resident. He noticed that the luxury of the palace walls and floors diminished here. Everything began to look more worn out. Then he suspected that they were being taken to the oldest section of the palace. They eventually reached a large, wooden door that Barric opened, revealing a curved, descending staircase.

Barric stepped aside and instucted, "Go down the stairs, please."

James and Dilliam were the last in the procession, so James asked Barric as they passed by, "It's the old tower, isn't it?"

Barric nodded. After he was sure the others couldn't hear, he inquired, "Why are you going with them? You don't have to."

"It's our duty," Dilliam replied.

"Well," Barric said with a faint smile, "you won't be getting the full treatment. He's told me to make sure everyone is fairly comfortable."

"Do you know what he's up to?" James asked.

Barric shook his head. "He's changed since you left. He constantly surprises me these days. He has a wisdom and shrewdness beyond his years, but at times he seems like a lost child."

The dungeon was as dark and damp as a dungeon could be. But the large cell in which they were placed had been given fresh straw, several pitchers of fresh water, and even a couple of bowls of fruit.

"This isn't so bad," Yon observed as he took off his gold coat and carefully folded it over an unused trough.

"Have you lost your mind?" Sesta growled at him. "Do you really think he's ever going to let us out of here?"

"Why is he doing this?" Fortawince asked. "What does he have to gain by locking us up? Surely he knows that Father will rally all of Marus to battle for our freedom."

This comment was met with silence. It was a lie and they all knew it. The people of Marus were in no condition to fight anyone, least of all Palatia.

"What do you make of this?" Drouse asked Dilliam.

"It's not for me to say," he answered.

"It is if we ask you!" Sesta shouted angrily.

Dilliam was unaffected by Sesta's outburst. He said, "You must search your own hearts. Is there something to be learned from this trouble?"

"Are you saying the Unseen One is responsible for this?" Cannap asked.

"Maybe He is and maybe He isn't," Dilliam said. "Sometimes we can't tell until *afterward.*"

"After we're dead, you mean," Naud replied with a wry chuckle.

Dilliam allowed silence to fill the cell again. They waited. He turned away from them with the words "Search your hearts."

CHAPTER TWENTY-ONE

The next morning, Barric came down to the dungeon. It was too soon for Selsond to have returned with Transe, so James knew something else was about to happen.

"The esteemed Glenn wants to meet with you," he announced.

They were taken back to the reception room. No sooner had they sat down, with Dilliam and James standing at the back again, than Glenn entered and took his seat under the canopy.

"I have reconsidered your case," he said pleasantly. "It was unreasonable to hold all of you while your brother comes. As a show of good faith, I will hold only one of you."

The brothers reacted favorably to this news—until it dawned on them that one would have to stay behind.

Glennall continued, "To demonstrate that I am not a harsh man, I will also send a gift to your father."

"A gift, my lord?" Rastall asked, surprised.

"Yes," Glennall said with a dramatic sweep of his hand. "I will send a gift of grain with you. Give it to your father with my compliments. And bring your youngest brother to me."

"What kind of game is he playing?" James whispered to Dilliam.

Dilliam shrugged.

"Now," Glennall stood up and pointed to Sesta, "I want *you* to stay while your other brothers go."

"Me, my lord?" Sesta asked, his expression pained.

"Yes." Glennall gestured to Barric and then strode out of the room.

"I will take you to your wagons, which we have brought from the tavern and loaded with grain," Barric stated, then waved to the guards. They walked over to Sesta to take him away.

"Wait!" Dilliam called out. Everyone stopped to hear him. "My apprentice and I will also stay with Sesta."

Barric looked slightly bemused. "If you wish," he agreed.

Dilliam and James went to Sesta's side, and they all left together.

Once they were secure in the dungeon again, Sesta turned on Dilliam and James. His face was flushed, and his eyes seemed to bulge from their sockets. "He's punishing me, isn't he?" he cried.

"What do you mean?" Dilliam asked.

Sesta began to pace, wringing his hands frantically. "Somehow he knows what happened to Glennall! You told him. Or the Unseen One told him. And he's punishing me for it."

"You'll have to explain yourself," Dilliam said.

Sesta picked up a bowl of fruit and threw it at Dilliam. Dilliam ducked aside. "Don't play your games with me!" Sesta thundered. "I'm sure the boy has told you what he saw! He knows what really happened to Glennall! In fact, he knows more than I do! What happened, boy? How did Glennall die? As a slave in some terrible Palatian camp?" Sesta began to weep uncontrollably. "Is that how it happened? Is that why I'm being punished now?"

Dilliam crossed the cell and put his huge arms around Sesta. Sesta stayed there a moment, like a small, lost boy, then suddenly pushed Dilliam away.

"No, no!" he cried. "It's too late for that! I don't deserve comfort. I want to feel the full penalty of what I've done." He went to the corner of the cell and slid into it, curled himself into a small ball, and began to rock from side to side. He stayed there, alternately weeping and rocking, for the next two days.

On the morning of their third day in the dungeon, Barric brought word that the brothers had returned with Transe.

Sesta stood up stiffly and left the cell without a word.

Barric held up his hand to stop James. "He sees it all, you know," he whispered.

"Glennall's been watching us in this dungeon?"

Barric nodded. "He's very confused. He's been having terrible, blinding headaches. I wish you'd speak to him now. I'm afraid he's about to crack up."

James looked to Dilliam. Dilliam looked away.

"Not yet," James said.

The brothers and Transe were in Glenn's reception room when Sesta, James, and Dilliam arrived. Once again the brothers took their seats while Dilliam and James stood at the back.

"We had to beg Father to let Transe go," Selsond told Sesta. "He says this whole thing is a curse. I thought watching us leave would kill him."

Drouse added, "If anything happens to Transe, it *will* kill him."

"I'll die first," Sesta said softly.

"Don't be so dramatic," Yon argued. "We've done what Glenn wants, and we got three wagons-full of grain in the bargain. It'll be all right now."

"No. It isn't that easy," Sesta insisted, his eyes tearing up again.

Rastall put a hand on Sesta's shoulder. "Are you all right?" he asked.

Sesta quickly beckoned his brothers together. They leaned forward like men in a huddle. "This is justice," he informed them. "This is our penalty for what we did to Glennall."

Some of the brothers gasped, some put their hands over their mouths, and Turnan hissed, "Keep your mouth shut, you fool!"

Transe looked confused. "Glennall?" he questioned. "What about Glennall?"

The door behind the platform opened just then, and Glenn entered and sat once again in the shadow of his canopy. Barric stood off to one side, watching them all carefully. Two guards were positioned near the doors.

Rastall stepped forward, his arm around Transe, and announced, "This is our youngest brother, my lord, as you requested."

Glennall stayed perfectly still. He didn't speak. It was hard for James to see what he was doing or what kind of expression he had on his face. When he finally spoke, he sounded hoarse, as if he had a cold. "I see" was all he said. He cleared his throat.

"Our father sends his gratitude for your gift of grain and hopes you may now be assured of our good intentions," Rastall continued. "With your permission, we would like to negotiate the purchase of more grain for our people."

Glennall suddenly clapped his hands together. "Negotiate we will! Let's adjourn to my private dining chamber, where we will eat and discuss our business." He stood up and left.

Barric opened the door and invited them all to follow him.

"Is that it?" James asked Dilliam. "Was that his revenge?"

Dilliam looked bewildered. "I honestly don't know," he replied.

The curtains in the dining chamber were drawn so that the room was dark. Candles were lit in holders on the wall and in the center of the table. *Another way to disguise himself,* James thought.

Glennall sat at the head of the table, with 13 settings of silver plates, cups, and cutlery for the rest of them. He insisted that Transe sit next to him. James, who was certain that Glennall was purposefully ignoring him, made it a point to sit at the opposite end from Glennall, along with Dilliam.

Glennall and Rastall talked business, with occasional interjections from some of the other brothers. They negotiated a cash price for the grain, much to James's surprise. Glennall never brought up the idea of food in exchange for land. James also noticed that Glennall asked a lot of questions about the family, especially Connam's health, and paid close attention to Transe, making sure he had plenty of food and drink.

No one but James and Dilliam seemed to notice Sesta. He sat quietly at his place, nibbling at his food, staring at the table in front of him.

When the meal had ended, Glennall stood up and closed a large ledger in which he'd been making notes. "I must go now," he said as if he were sorry to leave them. "Barric will show you to our royal treasurer to pay for the grain you wish to buy. I wish you well in your journey." With that said, he left the room.

The brothers looked at one another. They were mystified by this strange turn of events. To have gone from the dungeon to Glenn's favor seemed more than they could have hoped for.

"You see, Sesta?" Cannap said jovially, clapping his brother on the back. "The crisis is over."

Sesta didn't reply.

James wondered if it really was over and done with. After all this time hoping and praying for revenge, was Glennall really going to let them go? It didn't seem possible. And yet Barric had said that Glennall seemed terribly confused. Maybe he truly was heading for a breakdown.

"Or," Dilliam offered as they got into their wagon outside the palace door, "maybe he had the change of heart we have been praying for."

As they urged the horses on, James couldn't help but feel a sense of disappointment. He had thought he had a role to play. He had thought his presence was needed. Apparently he had been wrong.

The guard at the front gate of the palace called the convoy to a halt.

"Is something wrong?" Rastall asked him.

"We've been told to search your wagons," the guard answered.

Suddenly they were surrounded by palace guards. Then Chalcer, looking as dignified and threatening as ever, stepped from the guardhouse. He walked past James without looking at him, circled around the back of the wagons, and moved up the other side. He stopped next to Transe.

"What do you have in that bag?" he asked Transe.

"Which bag?" Transe asked with a nervous chuckle. "The wagons are full of bags of grain."

"The bag at your feet," Chalcer specified.

Transe looked down and picked up a satchel. "This isn't my bag," he protested. "I've never seen it before."

Chalcer took the satchel and opened it up. He pulled out a silver cup, a silver plate, silver cutlery—and the large ledger Glennall had been writing in during their meal. "Is this how you show your gratitude?" Chalcer asked accusingly.

"I don't know how those got there!" Transe said, his voice rising in tandem with his panic. "It must be a joke! I didn't take them!"

"A poor joke," Chalcer said coldly. "Arrest him. Put him in the dungeon."

"No!" Rastall cried and leapt from his wagon.

The guards held up their spears and muskets.

Rastall fell at Chalcer's feet. "If you're going to take anyone, take me," he begged. "Please!"

"Are you confessing to this theft?" Chalcer asked.

"No, but—"

"Then this is nothing to do with you."

Chalcer signaled the guards to take Transe to the dungeon. The boy began to weep as they dragged him away. He pleaded his innocence and begged his brothers to help him. Sesta fell to the ground and also wept, pounding his fists into the dirt.

"Punishment!" he wailed over and over.

Rastall stood up and began pacing back and forth, unsure of what to do. "This will kill our father!" he muttered. "How can I go back and face him? I gave him my word—my *word*—that we would return Transe safe and sound to him."

"Punishment!" Sesta lamented.

The rest of the brothers sat numbly, their mouths hanging open, their expressions dulled by the shock of it all.

"I've had enough of his games!" James announced suddenly. He climbed off the wagon and started marching toward the palace.

"What are you doing?" Rastall shouted after him.

James didn't answer but continued on.

"You'll get us *all* killed!" Naud yelled.

Distantly, James thought he heard Dilliam say to them, "He's the only one who can help you now."

CHAPTER TWENTY-TWO

———✦———

James walked around the palace to the side entrance. Barric was waiting for him there. "I saw you coming," he said.

"Where is he?" James demanded.

"Meeting with the king's governors. I think you should wait in his chambers."

"I'm not waiting another minute for him," James insisted and barreled on.

Barric followed him. "I'll be in trouble if I let you through."

"There's going to be trouble if you *don't* let me through. Which room is it?"

"The third door on the left." Barric's voice was receding. He had stopped where he was. "Good luck," he encouraged.

James didn't stop at the door but pushed it open as soon as he got to it. Glennall was sitting at a round table with six other men. They all had their heads down as they pored over ledgers and papers with their pens poised. James's entrance caused them all to look up.

"Well, well," Glennall said.

"We have to talk," James responded.

"Make an appointment with my secretary."

"*Now.*"

"I can have you arrested."

James dug into the inside pocket of his coat and pulled out an envelope. "I have a letter here with the king's seal that says otherwise."

A smile played at the corner of Glennall's mouth. He was impressed. "All right." He told the group of men, "We'll have to continue this later."

189

The men stood up and looked at James curiously as they paraded out. They were no doubt wondering how a boy could command the king's right-hand man like that. When they were gone, James stepped into the room and closed the door.

"Are you happy now?" James asked. "Are you happy with your revenge?"

Glennall stood up and went to the window. It overlooked the front lawn of the palace. "I see my brothers are still at the front gate," he said casually.

"Only because you planted that bag of goodies on Transe and put him in the dungeon."

Glennall rubbed his forehead. A red vein stuck out, like a worm under his skin. "They've all come true. All my dreams. I have risen above my brothers."

"Big deal."

Glennall paused for a moment, then half turned to him. "You left me, James. Just when we made it to the top."

"That wasn't as important to me as it was to you."

"You still left."

"You didn't need me anymore."

"You don't know that."

"Sure I do. I couldn't stomach what you were becoming," James said angrily. "I don't pretend to know much, but I *do* know that I didn't come here from my world to help you get revenge against your brothers."

"No? Then what did you come for?" Glennall shouted.

"To stop you."

"Stop me?" Glennall asked, astonished. "What makes you think you can stop me?"

James took a step toward him. "By showing you what's going to happen if you carry on this way." James stretched out his hand toward Glennall.

Glennall retreated a step. "What are you doing?"

"You said all your dreams have come true. Now let's join hands and see what new dreams are coming."

Glennall moved to the other side of the table. "Stay away."

"Why?" James asked, still moving toward him. "You were never afraid before. Why are you afraid now?"

"I'm not afraid."

"Then take my hand. Let's see what the Unseen One wants us to see."

"No."

"Why not?"

"I don't want to." Glennall continued to move unsteadily around the table with James following him. "Besides, you know it doesn't work that way."

"But it *might* work."

"Keep away."

"Are you afraid the Unseen One will show you something you don't want to see?"

"Why should I be afraid of that?"

"Because you don't really know the Unseen One anymore. You've lost sight of the whole point."

"That's insane."

James pressed on. "I've learned a lot from Brother Dilliam over the past few months. One thing I learned is that there's a big difference between the Unseen One you told me about and the Unseen One he's told me about."

"Dilliam was my mentor," Glennall argued. He rubbed his forehead again and stumbled against a chair. They kept going around and around. "Dilliam taught me everything I know."

"Then you forgot." James inched closer to Glennall. "The Unseen One I know is about love and justice all wrapped up into one. But you got the idea that He's all about power and revenge. That's all you've talked about since I met you."

"My brothers betrayed me. It was reasonable to think the Unseen One would make things right, raising me up so I could have my revenge."

"You got it half right, Glennall. The Unseen One *is* making things right, but not the way you think, and not so you can get revenge."

"Then why?"

"Think about it. He raised us both up while we were slaves, remember? But He raised us up so we could see what mercy was all about. It was like a rehearsal for the mercy we were supposed to show later. He put you in this position to show mercy."

Glennall repeated the word numbly: "Mercy."

"What your brothers did was wrong. They meant to hurt you. But the Unseen One used their evil for a greater good. You were put in this position to show the mercy of the Unseen One just like He showed us His mercy over and over."

"I've been showing mercy," Glennall said defensively, his conviction weakening. "Do you think any of us would be surviving this famine if I hadn't worked it out? I've been showing mercy to the whole world!"

"But you're not supposed to show it to just the whole world. You're supposed to show it to your *brothers*, too. Don't you see? This isn't about revenge; it's about mercy. It's not about getting even; it's about forgiveness. That's how the Unseen One has been making it right. He's been doing it all along."

Glennall gazed at James with red-rimmed eyes. "Why did you leave me? You were my conscience, James. None of this would've happened if you'd stayed."

"Yes, it would have. I couldn't have stopped you then. I wasn't strong enough. But things have changed. I understand the Unseen One better now. And I think you do, too."

"My faith in Him never faltered," Glennall affirmed softly.

"No, but you got confused about what He was doing. Now give me your hand."

"My head hurts," he said. "My headaches came back."

"Give me your hand."

"What will happen to me? Will the Unseen One do something to me?" His voice now reminded James of the kid he first met in the mine shaft. He sounded helpless and unsure.

James stopped their game of merry-go-round and held out his hand firmly. "You won't know until you give me your hand, Glennall."

Glennall also stopped where he was. "We were two halves of the same story, James," he said sadly.

"I know."

Glennall impulsively reached forward and took James's hand. He had no idea what would happen, but he knew beyond a shadow of a doubt that it was the right thing to do.

Suddenly the door opened. Chalcer looked in. "The traitors from Marus, your honor," he announced.

"You brought them to me?" Glennall asked, confused.

"I received a message that you wanted to see them."

Glennall looked at James, then down at their hands, still clasped. James wondered if somehow the Unseen One had communicated the idea to Chalcer. Why else would he bring the brothers to Glennall's office?

"What are you going to do?" James asked Glennall.

Glennall seemed to think about it, then ordered Chalcer, "Bring them in." He released James's hand.

Chalcer opened the door wide, and a guard led the brothers in. They looked pale and worried, but also surprised to see James standing so close to their accuser. The guard put the satchel on the table and opened it so the chalice, cutlery, and ledger could be seen.

"Bring the other one to us, the one you've taken to the dungeon," Glennall commanded as he quickly turned away from the room and looked out the window.

"Yes, your honor," Chalcer said and dismissed a guard to do the task.

Everyone stood silently. Glennall stayed with his back to them all and stared out the window with his hands clasped behind him. He stayed like a statue for the minutes that felt like hours. James wondered what was going through his mind.

Finally, Rastall cleared his throat and began, "Your honor, this is a grave error—"

Glennall held up his hand for silence.

Rastall lowered his head.

Eventually the guard returned with Transe, who blinked and looked to his brothers with a bewildered expression.

"Leave us, Chalcer, and take the guard with you," Glennall ordered, his back still turned to them all.

Chalcer looked puzzled. "But, your honor—"

"Leave us!" Glennall commanded more firmly.

Chalcer bowed stiffly and signaled to the guard, and they retreated, closing the door behind them.

The brothers watched Glennall with undisguised fear. Anything could happen to them now, and they knew it. Even James wasn't entirely sure what Glennall would do next.

"My brothers," Glennall began, and then he stopped as his voice suddenly choked with emotion. He turned to face them, the light from the window splashing onto his face. He undid his royal robe and dropped it to the floor, now standing before them in a simple tunic.

James saw the brothers shift uneasily. Sesta's eyes grew

wide, as if he couldn't believe what he was seeing. In the light, with the robe gone, the great Glenn looked familiar. He looked remarkably like Glennall.

The rest of the brothers must have thought the same thing, for they also gazed wide-eyed, their mouths dropping open.

Glennall took a deep breath to control the tears that wanted to come. "My brothers, come to me!" he cried. "Look closely!"

Mystified, the brothers obeyed and moved around the table, venturing closer and closer.

"I am Glennall, your brother."

Sesta's eyes filled with tears, and his lips trembled. He fell to his knees at Glennall's feet. "May the Unseen One forgive me!" he wept.

Glennall grabbed his brother's arms and drew him to his feet. "No, brother. Do not bow, and do not reproach yourself. Though you were wrong, the Unseen One has made all things right. Embrace me and know that … that …" Glennall stammered for a moment and shot a quick glance at James. "Know that all is forgiven."

Glennall could contain himself no longer and burst into tears, embracing Sesta, and then the rest of his brothers in turn. James decided it was time to slip out of the room, to let the family have their reunion in privacy.

Dilliam was also in the hall. They smiled at each other but didn't speak. There was nothing to say.

On the other side of the door, James could hear Glennall and his brothers weeping and talking and even laughing. Then, after the better part of an hour, Rastall came out, his face wet with tears. "I'm to fetch my father," he said and raced off.

"I'll go with you," Dilliam called after Rastall. Then he told James, "My work here is done. It's time I went home."

"Don't leave!" James pleaded. "Not yet."

Dilliam approached James and lightly touched his head. "God be with you on *your* journey," he replied in blessing.

Dilliam turned and walked down the hall. When he reached the end, he suddenly turned to face James again.

James wondered about this, but the door opened again and Glennall came out alone. "Don't stand here, James. Come inside," he invited. "We're going to have a feast, a celebration."

"I guess you're feeling better," James observed.

Glennall nodded. "Thank you for reminding me of what I knew all along but had chosen to forget." He reached out and touched James's hand. "Thank you."

A bright flash of light blinded them. James winced, and Glennall cried out. The hallway disappeared around them. When their vision cleared, they found themselves standing in the middle of a field.

Glennall blinked. "Where are we?"

James looked down at his feet. There were two rows of ruts in the soft dirt, the ruts of wagon wheels. "This is my field," he realized. "This is where it started."

Glennall looked pained. "What does it mean?"

James felt his heart rise in his throat. "I think it means I'm going home."

"But you can't!" Glennall begged. "Your world isn't your home anymore. *This* is your world. You belong in Marus. We're going to have great adventures together."

James wanted to stay. He wanted it more than anything in his life. "I don't think the Unseen One is going to let me stay," he answered, his voice shaking.

"But you have to!" Glennall held on to James's hand. "You can't go."

James thought he remembered something. It was a scene of Glennall being embraced by his father and a ring being taken from a locked box and placed upon Glennall's finger. But it wasn't the younger Glennall; it was Glennall as he was now.

James was "remembering" something that hadn't happened yet. Time was out of joint, he realized. He was still standing in the field with Glennall.

"You can't go! This is your home now!" Glennall pleaded, as if by saying it, it would become true.

"I know," James agreed. "If I can ever come back, I will."

"But what am I going to do until then?"

A mist seemed to come from nowhere and surround them. In one direction, just over Glennall's shoulder, James could see the hallway where he and Glennall had been a few moments before. Dilliam still stood at the end of it. He seemed to be watching them.

"Brother Dilliam will help you now," James stated.

James glanced back, in the opposite direction from the hallway. A police car sat on a distant road. Two officers stood next to it, looking at him.

"I think we're going to have to let go now," James said, his heart breaking.

The mist engulfed them.

"You'll come back," Glennall maintained, his grip on James's hand relaxing.

James knew he was about to sob, and he couldn't bear for Glennall to see it, so he opened his hand completely. The mist covered his face, thick as cotton wool.

Glennall was gone.

James stood in the middle of the field alone.

The stern voice of a policeman called out to him. But this time James didn't run.

EPILOGUE

———✦———

Whit and Jack sat at the counter of Whit's End and said nothing. They were lost in their own thoughts. Connie, who was now perched on a stool, gazed at the two men. The air was full of sunset and the night to come.

Whit touched the cover of the notebook gently. "So that's the story of James Curtis," he finally said.

"Amazing," Connie replied. "But it doesn't mean the story is *true*."

Neither man answered.

"Look," she continued, "it was a really good story, and I can see why you guys are so intrigued. But be honest now. You don't *really* think there's another world called Marus, do you?"

Whit looked at her but didn't respond.

"Jack?" she asked.

Jack shrugged and took a sip from his coffee mug.

"Oh, come on. Don't do that to me!" she complained to both of them. "It's a simple question with a simple answer."

"Is it?" Whit asked.

"Yes!" she insisted.

"Maybe it isn't," Whit said. "And maybe we'll find out when we meet James Curtis tomorrow morning."